HOSTAGE!

HOSTAGE!

BY JAMES HAMILTON - PATERSON

COLLINS

New York and Cleveland

First published in the United States of America
by William Collins Publishers, Inc.
New York and Cleveland, 1980.
Copyright © 1978 by James Hamilton-Paterson.
(First published in Great Britain
by Victor Gollancz, Ltd., 1978)
All rights reserved.
Printed in the United States of America.

Library of Congress Cataloging in Publication Data

Hamilton-Paterson, James.
  Hostage!
    SUMMARY: Mistakenly kidnapped by a guerilla
group, the son of an American oil executive discovers
that as the weeks of his captivity pass he is less and
less sure which side he wants to be on.
  [1. Kidnapping—Fiction. 2. Terrorism—Fiction]
I. Title.
PZ7.H18285Hn 1980   [Fic]   79-25114
ISBN 0-529-05596-1

For Alice, Cathy, David and Kevin, who can recognize Zibala when they see it.

Chapter 1

Monday was the day they usually went riding out at Assuf. The Embassy car, a vast ginger Chevrolet with diplomatic plates, collected Wayne after lunch. Bernard was sitting in one corner at the back, his legs turned sideways and elegantly crossed as if to emphasize the spaciousness. He was wearing an old pair of Levi's tucked into shabby cowboy boots. He looked terrific.

"So," he said as the car pulled away, "what happened at lunch?" He turned his head to glance out of the window as he spoke. Wayne recognized the question as not requiring a serious answer since Bernard would not be listening.

"Nothing much except that some men dropped a Butagas cylinder in the street and it exploded. You know, their usual trick of rolling them off the back of the truck onto a heap of sacking. I suppose the cylinders had been well baked in the sun anyhow and all it needed was the extra knock. They're always doing it. One of the men got some metal in his wrist and Ali came rushing in to my mother shouting that a bomb had gone off. He thought it was the start of a revolution or something because he went on about *Bolshevik* until my mother . . ."

"I should take the Wadi Ain route, Hassan," Bernard sang out suddenly in French. "We're a bit pressed for time since our late start." Yards away up front the driver inclined his head. "Sorry, Wayne," said Bernard in English once more. "Do go on, how interesting. We really ought to be at the stables by three because otherwise all the best horses go. I'm sure I told you about last week when I went riding with the Turkish Prime Minister's son. They had obviously forgotten to ring up and Mumtaz took such a time to dress that by the time we got there the decent mounts were being flogged to death by a party of German tourists and there were only a handful of nags left. Listen, I made quite a fuss as you can imagine; I think Mumtaz was pretty surprised. Prime Minister's son or no Prime Minister's son he's not too effective when it comes to getting his own way. While I did the talking he just wandered off, all dolled up in his English gentleman's kit carrying a little ivory crop with emeralds in the handle. I'm sure he's gay and I could see he didn't cut much ice with the *mudir*. I finally told the *mudir* that unless he brought out a couple of decent horses for us in the next five minutes there would be a scene he wouldn't forget and that I would personally guarantee the entire diplomatic community was warned off his stables. Well, surprise, surprise, within thirty seconds a kid came out leading a couple of superb Arabs . . ."

Bernard was well away now and, Wayne knew, would keep it up until they reached Assuf. He turned his head away with a mixture of disquiet and envy, anxious not to meet the boy's blue gaze. Bernard Levesque (he pronounced his first name French fashion, *Bare-narr*, since his family were French Canadians from Quebec) was by default the most important person in Wayne's life. From the moment they had met as thirteen-year-old classmates in the American School of al-Mazar, Bernard had completely eclipsed Wayne's own parents. He had done so by the same degree with which he—as the son of Quebec's Ambassador to Zibala—surpassed them socially. Now, two years later, Wayne acknowledged that Bernard seemed to outweigh his own father in every other respect as well. Such was the mingled admiration and resentment he felt for Bernard that Wayne found nothing strange in considering his fifteen-year-old friend superior to a man twenty-eight years his senior. They were in different leagues.

". . . so Dad is going to sweet-talk Gallimard into letting me go to the Lycée there because frankly the College here is just full of jerks who aren't going anywhere, and after the *Bac*. I think a business degree at Harvard might be quite useful. Or Oxford, even, since Dad's close friends with the Dean of one of the colleges. What do you think?"

The car was passing a smoking and battered bus so crammed with people that it was lopsided. Boys and young men clung to the outside as it roared along, horn blaring. A donkey cart appeared suddenly on the center island of the four-lane highway and wandered off into the fast lane in front of them. Hassan braked violently, leaning on the horn. The driver of the cart, a peasant with a lined brown face, was lying full length among his vegetables, head propped on one hand, eyes closed and the reins held limply in his other hand. The donkey clearly knew the way home of its own accord for it went plodding on across both lanes, missing the bus by centimeters, and up over the broken pavement.

"Jerk," said Bernard. "Don't tell me he looked. Did you see him? He was fast asleep. And look at that traffic cop. What a country."

Hassan's evasive action had taken the Embassy car to the edge of the curb. Sitting on a chair on a splintered wooden dais was a middleaged policeman, a picturebook propped on his lap and a stub of pencil between his teeth. Wayne recognized the book as Book I of the Government reading primer used in schools and sold on the streets everywhere as part of Zibala's literacy drive.

"I expect he's studying for the Harvard entrance exam," said Wayne as Hassan accelerated away again. Here on the outskirts near Assuf the traffic was far better than in the city center. As the road approached the fringe of the desert so it became clearer. The shops and apartment blocks had gradually given way to single-story mud-brick houses, flat-roofed and whitewashed, interspersed with large pastel villas sporting neon signs on their roofs which said "Casino." These were not gambling dens at all but simply night clubs and restaurants. The Arabs, properly conscious of the wealthy tourists who flocked in winter pilgrimage to the ruins and monuments of Assuf, had given their establishments a name which might conjure up the world of elegant high living the homesick westerners had left. Wayne had been to such casinos on several occasions with his parents, but their garish promise was always belied by the reality of overpriced meals served kindly but incompetently in big pink rooms, followed several hours later by agonizing diarrhea.

The huge bulk of the ruined Temple of Shamm appeared. Bernard leaned forward onto the back of the front seat, chin on his bare brown forearms. "You'll wait for us, won't you, Hassan?" he said in French.

"*D'accord, M'sieur.*"

"You don't mind, do you? The car's not needed: I checked."

"Of course not, sir."

"He can always go drink a glass of tea or play back-gammon with the stable hands," explained Bernard in English as if to himself. "Or sleep," he added.

The car turned off the road and began bumping down a track. Under a group of palms about twenty camels were tethered and behind them were the tattered sand-colored tents of the Zibalan army. Several soldiers lay like corpses in the shade; one was dozing with his head propped against his kneeling camel's flank. Three more sat at a table beside the track nodding over glasses of tea. Since they were guarding the road against a surprise attack by Israelis, Hassan slowed the car in a token gesture and called a greeting through his window as they went by. One of the guards raised his hand in reply, his companions stared.

"Jerks," said Bernard lazily.

The ruins of Shamm, like most places of Zibala of the least interest, were designated a military zone and officially special passes were required for visits to any of them. However, in deference to the foreign tourists whose money the Zibalan economy needed, this rule was waived except in times of National Crisis (on average once every two months) or in the remoter desert sites where the local army commander wanted the visitor's fee to buy cigarettes.

Presently the car stopped and the boys got out. Wayne spied the *mudir* picking his nose just inside his office, a whitewashed mud-brick hut on the front wall of which was written "God is great" in Arabic script and "Best stables in the midle-est" in English underneath. Seeing Bernard, the *mudir* hurried out, wiping his finger on the neck of a tethered horse on the way.

"Welcome, Excellency," said the *mudir*, seizing Bernard's hand. As an afterthought he offered his hand to Wayne as well, but his eyes remained fixed on Bernard's face.

"Are there any decent horses left?" demanded Bernard, scanning the row of stable doors over several of which drooped large equine heads.

"Of course, sir," the manager assured him. "All my horses here are tip-top, as the English say. It is true, some are tip-topper than others. But that is right because we have horses for everyone. For you and your friend"—he glanced at Wayne—"only the best, as usual. Now, how far you go today? How long you want? You go perhaps Ramla? Tombs of Hundred Kings?"

"How do you feel, Wayne?" asked Bernard. "Are we energetic enough to go all the way to Ramla and back before dark?"

"Why not?" said Wayne. "We're early, it's not too hot and we haven't been for ages."

The *mudir* brightened. He hired his horses by the hour. Four Zibalan pounds, plus tip, say four-fifty . . .

"And no guide," added Bernard firmly. "We're quite good

enough horsemen not to need a nanny, as you well know. In any case we know the way."

The *mudir* let his face fall. "No guide"—he shook his head doubtfully—"It is not good two young sirs go in the desert alone on my tip-toppest horses without guide." It was a little ritual which had to be played out. Another fifty for letting them out without a guide . . .

"Five pounds," said Bernard.

"*Mabrouk*," agreed the *mudir* happily. He shouted an order and a boy appeared leading a pair of saddled horses. "My tip-toppest," said the *mudir*.

Bernard walked all around them, running a hand knowledgeably down a fetlock here, looking at a mouth there. Wayne watched uneasily, hoping he would not find fault. To break the silence he stepped forward and took the nearest bridle. "They don't look bad at all, Bernard," he said. "I've never seen this one before but I've ridden the one you're holding. He's good and lively."

"Oh, yes," said Bernard. "Yes, I've ridden him, too. He isn't bad except that he looks as though he could do with a square meal. That one you've got is the better of the two."

"Very good horse," said the *mudir*, "I get him yesterday."

"You have him," urged Wayne. "I'm happy with the other one."

"No, no," insisted Bernard. "You take him. You're probably a better rider than I am anyway," he said without conviction. "At least I know from experience that I can handle old bony here."

The ruins of Ramla lay perhaps ten miles away. A guide was hardly necessary in order to find them since they were clearly visible across what seemed to be a flat expanse of stony desert. The famous four towers—immense cylindrical structures in pale yellow stone—rose up on the horizon reminding Wayne unromantically of the cooling towers of a power station near where his aunt lived in England. They had the same waisted shape although the tombs at Ramla were capped with round domes.

Although they were so famous they were not much visited by tourists passing through al-Mazar, the Zibalan capital. Al-Mazar itself was founded on an old dynastic city and there were plenty of ruins to be found within easy walking distance of its Hilton and Sheraton hotels. Moreover, the trip to Ramla was notorious for its discomfort. Some geological event in the timeless past had left the ten miles between al-Mazar and Ramla a contorted wasteland of gullies, dunes and rocky outcrops which could only be negotiated by Land Rover or other four-wheel-drive vehicles. The air-conditioned tourist buses had many times tried and failed to make the journey, having to be winched out of difficulties by Zibalan army vehicles and on one occasion needing to be pushed through a deep drift of sand by its perspiring passengers—elderly men from South Dakota with heart conditions and their wives with blue rinses and Polaroid sunglasses on lanyards around their necks.

Consequently it had been accepted that the only way to reach Ramla was in acute discomfort or on horseback, and this trip alone had done much to confirm Zibala's reputation among travel agencies as being of Grade H toughness. Grade A described the most accessible and comfortable European resorts while, for example, Grade D was reserved for the adventurous at heart who wanted romantic locations but who could put up with rather less luxury. Grade H was frankly horrific and applied only to Zibala and a collection of ruins in the Yucatan peninsula of Mexico where an intrepid party of twenty tourists had once been raped and dismembered by a passing band of bored Indians.

"How's the horse?" asked Bernard as they picked their way down a narrow defile.

"Not bad. Very soft mouth and eager to go. What about yours?"

"As usual. I'd forgotten this one." It was like sitting on a moving heap of coathangers. "Still, isn't it nice to be out of al-Mazar? It's so quiet. Great not to have anybody yelling and screaming at you."

Al-Mazar had, over the previous ten years, gradually become less fit for human beings to live in. Its population had quadrupled and little had been built but apartments for the rich and office blocks for the foreign companies who were hopefully going to descend on Zibala any day to take advantage of the economic boom the President promised was just around the corner. The city was overcrowded, filthy, smelly and noisy. The telephones scarcely worked, the few postmen could not read, public transport ran on a shoestring. Large areas of the city were left without electricity or water or both at irregular hours of day or night. Some side streets were entirely blocked by rubbish, and the city itself lay beneath an immense dark stain of pollution which could be seen seventy miles away across the desert. Those who could afford it took every opportunity of escaping from al-Mazar.

Bernard was right, Wayne thought as he allowed his horse to pick its own path across a patch of terrain which looked like the magnified surface of a piece of flapjack. It was particularly good to get away from the ever-present voices shouting, abusing, selling, demanding, or just chanting passages from the Koran over faulty loudspeakers. It was not until they had convinced the *mudir* of the stables that they were competent and reliable that the boys had been allowed out together without a "guide" to make sure they did not overtire the horses or gallop them at breakneck speed down rocky gullies. Until then, their every excursion had been shadowed by a robed and turbaned figure, who had once suddenly and without warning exposed himself when they were resting the horses. Wayne had looked up to see him standing motionless on a small outcrop a few yards away, silhouetted against the sky. The man was grinning hugely;

but what Wayne remembered most clearly was that one of his ears had been pierced for a thick earring, and through the hole, a tiny circle of blue sky was visible.

Now he watched Bernard moving along a ridge above him and to his right, a slender figure casually graceful in his boots and faded jeans, sitting his horse with an ease which Wayne knew he would never match. A familiar pang shot through him, followed—and how familiar this was, too!—by the painfully clear image of how he himself looked: the fat thighs forced apart by his horse's back, his checked shirt deliberately not tucked into his trousers so that its loose folds hid the roll of white tummy which overhung his belt, his thatch of mousy hair. Wayne hated his body for the way in which it so neatly betrayed him. He had once believed he had a destiny to be lean and brown, but life conspired to cheat him of that destiny.

Convinced that even his plumper contemporaries at school looked better because they had a tan, he now and again embarked on a campaign of furtive sunbathing. But it was difficult to arrange it so that he was not seen. After investigation Wayne had decided that the only possible place was on the roof at home: a flat-tiled area covered with drifts of dust which nobody ever visited. On the first occasion he had waited until both his parents were safely out for a few hours before going up to the roof with a large towel on which to lie, a bottle of suntan lotion and a book. Before he could spread the towel out, however, a patch had to be swept clear. The noise of his sweeping had brought their servant Ali puffing up the stairs. Ali had clearly thought Wayne mad. No foreigner swept roofs, and in any case the idea of lying exposed to the sun struck any Arab as purest insanity. Moreover, Ali seemed rather put out by it all, perhaps because he saw an insult in Wayne's doing his job.

When he had finally got rid of him, Wayne had locked the door, stripped to his underwear, lathered himself in oil and flopped out on the towel. He lay on his stomach with sweat

pouring in runnels down either side of his nose until he could
bear it no longer, then turned over onto his back. A sudden
laugh froze him. Squinting against the sunlight, he made out
the outlines of two Zibalan women watching him from the
overlooking roof of a block of flats. Dumb women, he
thought in an anguish of embarrassment, getting to his feet
and dragging the towel protectively around him. Why the
hell are they messing around on the damned roof at this
time? Why don't they just drop dead?

As he retreated downstairs, Wayne knew it was of course
perfectly reasonable for the girls to have been on the roof. As
a matter of fact they lived there in a series of little shacks just
as thousands of Zibalan servants lived on the roofs of the
apartments they tended. Whole families lived on the
rooftops of al-Mazar with their chickens and sheep and goats
and huge piles of fodder. However, it struck Wayne as just
his luck that the roof of his own house was about as secluded
as a circus ring. Since then, he had stealthily tried again on
several occasions, even going so far as to erect a screen of
deck chairs against prying eyes. But his impatience to get as
much sun as possible before his parents came home led him
to overdo it badly. He went red, he peeled, he itched. On one
occasion he made the mistake of falling asleep on his
stomach. When he awoke, he knew at once he had gone too
far. The sun had caught the backs of his knees so that by
dinner time he could barely straighten his legs. Instead of
being as brown as a berry and carefree with his new body,
Wayne had been partially crippled for a fortnight. His lean
brown destiny was foiled again.

His horse stumbled and he looked up. They were nearing
Ramla, the four towers rising massively ahead out of a low
tumble of ruined archways, porticoes and temples. He and
Bernard had made the trip three times previously but Wayne
never tired of the place with its silence and immense
desolation. He hoped there would not be many tourists, but
as the horses picked their way neatly over the remains of the

outer wall of the great courtyard, Wayne saw that the place was empty. There were no vehicles parked in front of the wooden hut which sold bleached and curling postcards and bottles of warm Zibacola. Indeed, the hut itself was shut and the handful of guides nowhere to be seen. No doubt snoozing in the shade somewhere, thought Wayne as he followed Bernard over to a well shaded by a cluster of date palms. They dismounted.

"Strange," said Bernard, easing the crotch of his jeans, "we seem to have the place to ourselves. I can't believe it."

"It can't last. But I suppose if they don't want to earn their living, we'll just have to water the horses ourselves. Lazy bums, I bet they're all asleep." Wayne let down the parched leather bucket into the well and presently winched it up again brimming with water.

"I've never seen the place like this before," said Bernard.

"No, it's pretty sinister, isn't it?" agreed Wayne.

Even though the late March sun was more than three-quarters of its way across the sky, the glare which filled the vast courtyard was still considerable. The towers shimmered in the empty heat; nothing moved but the slow whisk of their horses' tails as they drank and no sound could be heard save that of their drinking. When they had done, the boys tethered them to a couple of palms.

"Well, let's take advantage of it," said Bernard. "I vote we climb one of the towers."

Visitors were strictly forbidden to go up the towers unless they paid the guides heavily to look the other way. It seemed an opportunity not to be missed. The dynastic inhabitants of Ramla had built the four towers as tombs for their kings. The oldest was roughly four thousand years old, and the most recent was scarcely less ancient, since the period of the great kingdoms had apparently lasted only a few hundred years. Little was known about the people who had flourished so long ago and for such a comparatively short time. It was clear that their religion had centered on their king, however,

since what few inscriptions had survived indicated that they
believed him to have been immortal. Indeed, the Ramlans
had only ever had one king—their first—whom they held to
have been reincarnated again and again in his successors. For
this reason the first and earliest tomb had a name on it, that of
Sukh. All the rest were completely anonymous, posing an
insoluble problem to archaeologists trying to match
references in the writings of other pre-Christian Middle
Eastern civilizations. All the kings were Sukh, or only one of
them was, nobody knew for sure.

Inside each tower a smooth ramp ascended like a
corkscrew to a point halfway up. The tombs of the kings led
off this ramp, built into the walls at regular intervals. Each
(except Sukh's) was unmarked; each was empty but for a
plain stone sarcophagus; and each sarcophagus itself
contained nothing but a single baked clay tablet with an
inscription which had been translated as "We wept." The
towers held twenty-five tombs apiece, but in the last only
sixteen of them contained sarcophagi. Scholars surmised
that the Ramlan civilization had collapsed before all the
tombs could be filled. The foundations for a fifth tower had
been laid and were still visible, but whatever tragedy had
overtaken this lost civilization had brought all further
building to a halt. Thus, although there had seemingly only
ever been ninety-one, the site was known as the Tombs of
the Hundred Kings.

Bernard and Wayne made their way across to the nearest
tower. It was nearly two hundred feet high to the top of its
dome and roughly half that wide at the base. Wayne thought
again of their incongruous resemblance to a row of cooling
towers. Their shape—slightly narrower in the middle than at
the top and bottom—was, he knew, a singular feat of
engineering. The immense blocks of masonry fitted so well
that the joints were still invisible in places, despite four
thousand years of eroding desert winds. The walls soared up

in a pure sweeping curve of yellow stone. The entrance was a plain rectangular doorway. Inside, the ascending ramp and its tombs took no account of the tower's external shape but went up in a regular wide spiral leaving a deep well of air in the middle. Guard rails had been erected all the way up the ramp after enough tourists had stumbled and tripped their way into wheelchairs and coffins, the circular platform at the top being a hundred feet above the stone floor.

Bernard and Wayne waited a moment for their eyes to adjust to the comparative gloom. The silence was intense, and it was noticeably cooler inside. There was a smell like the interior of a pottery jar. Underfoot a light dusting of sand had blown in from the desert along with a cigarette carton or two and the yellow foil wrapper from a roll of film. At the foot of the ramp were three empty Zibacola bottles. Bernard suddenly set off at a lope, running lightly on his toes up the ramp, around and around and higher and higher. Defeated, Wayne stood in the center of the floor, turning slowly on his heels to watch as Bernard grew smaller, circling upwards. The soft pad of his footsteps echoed down the central well, as regular and unflagging as the distant beating of carpets. He vanished into the upper gloom.

Wayne followed slowly, often pausing to peer into the black doorways of the tombs he passed so that if Bernard were watching from the top he would see there was a reason for his measured ascent. Wayne had no intention of arriving out of breath. Even so he was sweating freely when he finally emerged onto the circular floor. He found Bernard sitting in the embrasure of one of the four slit-like windows which girdled the waist of the tower and which allowed some light to filter into its upper reaches. He was staring out towards al-Mazar over the terrain they had just crossed. Joining him, Wayne could see the distant city beneath its acid brown pall.

"Strange, I thought I saw someone moving out there," said Bernard, jabbing a finger downwards.

"Where?" asked Wayne. He wanted to ask more, but his heart was thumping in his throat from his recent climb and he was afraid it would jog his voice.

"Just behind those rocks to the left of that patch of sand."

Wayne followed the pointing finger but could see nothing. "Who was it, a tourist?"

"No, definitely not a tourist. I only caught a quick glimpse, but I think he looked more like a soldier. He could have had a gun." They waited a minute or two but nothing stirred in the desert outside. "Oh, well, perhaps I imagined it."

Wayne looked at him sitting in the embrasure, the sun lighting up his fair hair. It looked so like frayed silk that for a moment Wayne was seized with the desire to reach out and touch it to see if it was real. Perhaps Bernard wore a wig. Perhaps, come to that, he applied his tan carefully from a bottle at night in the bathroom. He glanced upwards into the semidarkness. The topmost hundred feet or so of the tower rose sheer. There was no ramp. Instead, a spiral of single stone slabs had been built into the masonry. The thin steps jutted out of the wall a couple of feet, each independent like a single tooth. They circled the full width of the central wall, for now there were no more tombs. There was no handrail, either, for tourists were absolutely forbidden to venture beyond this upper floor.

It so happened that Wayne was not afraid of heights. Without the least reason for feeling confident in his physical abilities, he none the less felt oddly secure in high places. He was unaffected by vertigo; he had no desire to hurl himself down; he was entirely certain he would not be enticed over the edges of the cliffs or off the tops of monuments by the horrid magnetism which his schoolmates claimed to feel pulling them towards their doom.

"I'm going on up," he said to Bernard. "Are you coming?"

Bernard too glanced upwards. "Are you mad?" he asked. "That's a hell of a way up. You're not seriously thinking of going up those steps, are you?" he added incredulously.

"You must be out of your mind. When I said we'd go up the towers, I only meant up to here, not right to the very top."

"Oh, I always meant to go up to the dome, of course," said Wayne. He suddenly felt an unaccustomed confidence. "It'll be our only chance. You're not bothered by heights, are you?" he asked slyly.

Bernard ignored the question. "Suppose you fell?" he said.

"I won't," said Wayne. "Why would I do a silly thing like that?"

"I don't mean on purpose," said Bernard crossly. "I mean suppose one of those steps was loose or broke off. They've been there four thousand years, you know. It's an idiotic idea."

"If they've stayed up that long, then they're probably good for another four thousand," said Wayne gaily. "Anyway, I'm going up. You don't have to come if you don't want to."

"You're damn right I won't. And neither will you." Suddenly Bernard's voice took on an imperious cutting edge which Wayne recognized with annoyance from countless scenes in which he had unwillingly witnessed the diplomat's son asserting his will over someone else and usually getting his own way. On such occasions Bernard sounded about four times his age, querulous and elderly. Wayne had once heard two of his teachers referring to him as "Monsieur Ego," and much as Bernard doted on school gossip Wayne had never quite been able to pass this piece on. Bernard's revenges were cold and ruthless and, Wayne felt without the slightest evidence, might even extend to getting someone fired.

"You are not to go up there, Wayne," he was saying. "It's extremely stupid. If you do, I shall be seriously annoyed."

Wayne began laughing, far more angered by his friend's tone than by the likelihood of being thwarted. "Don't be so pompous," he said. "If I want to go up, why shouldn't I? I'm not asking you to come up, too."

"Look," said Bernard with a kind of heavy reasonableness, "I don't want the responsibility . . ."

"Oh, great," said Wayne. "That's just great. All of a sudden you're responsible for me, is that it?"

"Yes it is," cried Bernard. "You fall and break your stupid leg and whose responsibility is it to get you back to al-Mazar? I mean let's face it, you're a real athlete, aren't you, Bulky?"

Wayne felt himself freeze, and then, his face suddenly hot, he began silently to climb. It was the first time in their two-year friendship that Bernard had used the hated school nickname. The betrayal was somehow very shocking and brought furious tears to his eyes. Despite them, he went on walking nimbly around the walls from stone to stone, ignoring the ever-increasing gulf opening up on his left hand. There was a silence; then Bernard's voice came up from below.

"Look, I'm sorry, Wayne," he said. "I didn't mean to say that. It's just that . . . You're okay. I mean, I *like* you, for heaven's sake, you know that . . ." Bernard was clearly having difficulty. He was standing in the middle of the dimly-lit floor, his face turned upwards like a pale sunflower, making Gallic gestures with his hands as words of affection failed him. "*T'es un brave mec*, Wayne. You make me laugh . . . I mean, you're funny. You're funnier than anyone else I know. Nobody else can make your sort of jokes . . ."

Still climbing and already about fifty feet up, Wayne made no reply, concentrating on where he was putting his feet while below him Bernard blundered on and on.

"Please come down," came his voice from below with a novel strain of entreaty. "Please, Wayne. I really think we ought to go . . . *Je t'en supplie* . . . If we leave it any later, the sun'll set before we get back."

"I won't be long," called down Wayne between strides. "Nearly there."

"Ah, *merde*," said Bernard, exasperated. "I can't watch

this. You're so bloody stubborn. I'm going down. I might wait for you at the bottom if I feel like it." He began going reluctantly down the ramp. But for their footsteps silence fell in the great tomb as the two friends unwound away from each other, spiralling towards their respective ends of the tower.

By the time he reached the top Wayne was sweating and breathing heavily, and not merely on account of the exertion. He squeezed sideways through the little porthole by the top step which led to the parapet outside. As he did so, he glanced back and was aware of being perched on the rim of a deep pit. Had any of the stone steps come loose, as Bernard had surmised and as his own imagination had pictured to him every inch of the way up, there would indeed have been little hope. Far below he could see the circular floor lit by four patches of sunlight from the windows and with a dark hole to one side which was the top of the ramp.

Outside the sunlight was dazzling, but once his eyes had adjusted, he saw that the view was incomparably better than it had been from halfway up. He squatted with his back firmly against the hot sandstone dome and with his feet wedged behind the parapet, recovering his breath. To his extreme left were the other towers, the dome of the nearest being exactly level with him and apparently only a good leap away, although he knew it was at least a hundred yards. On the other side the distant city had come into even better view; he could now distinguish individual landmarks. The capital's grotesque radio and television tower was clearly visible, as was the Sheraton Hotel. If he really screwed his eyes up, Wayne imagined for an instant that he could make out a smudge on top of the Ministry of News which in reality was a huge metal mesh supporting a neon sign. The neon sign blinked on and off all night and was so mysteriously unaffected by power cuts that a TWA captain had once told Wayne that pilots landing at al-Mazar Airport found it more reliable than the airport beacon. The sign itself simply said "Ramla" in English and Arabic script, this being the name of the most popular brand of cigarette.

Gingerly craning forward, Wayne peered over the edge beyond his toes. The two-hundred-foot drop was made even more sheer by the tower's shape: the overhang gave him the impression of sitting on an island in the air. Only about three-quarters of the way down did the outcurving yellow wall come into view. He turned his head. Their horses were invisible beneath the palm grove but he could see the well. For a moment he thought something flashed briefly among the rocks nearby, but when he stared more closely, he could see nothing. A broken bottle, even an exposed seam of mica, anything, he thought vaguely, except that a sudden gleam implied movement. The sun getting lower, perhaps. He wondered where Bernard was waiting. Well, let him wait a bit, he thought; it'll make a change. Might even do Monsieur Ego some good.

Wayne let his eyes wander down to his knees, unfocusing until his kneecaps themselves formed twin domes blotting out most of the landscape. Fat knees, he thought; repulsive fat knees. How he hated that nickname Bernard had used and which he now could not bring himself even to voice inwardly. Why was he so fat while he could see every muscle on Bernard's body? And Bernard ate like a pig, too: endless embassy food, informal dinners and receptions to which he was often invited if the other diplomats were friends of his family. At school the next day they would all hear about it: dishes whose names had an almost legendary gourmet ring since nobody else knew quite what they were: *quenelles* and *tournedos* and *saltimboccas* and *crêpes*. Plus, of course, Bernard's accounts of the social gossip of the mighty: the studied rudeness of outgoing Ambassador X towards incoming Ambassador Y; the crises which never got into the press when the spoiled brats of diplomats were caught at airports and frontiers with their pockets full of hash; the suicide of this or that foreign secretary for being found in compromising circumstances in a cabana reserved for Boy Scouts. All these were familiar to Wayne.

Yet it was not for the meals and the social chitchat he envied Bernard: it was for the automatic assumption that his life of privilege could be relied on to turn itself into hard cash as soon as he left school. Without lifting a finger, Bernard would become what he called "an entrepreneur" (and what on earth *did* that mean?); or he would be the personal aide to some prime minister or other whose godson he happened to be. Bernard would become an "adviser," an "assistant," an "aide." Monsieur Ego would become Young Mr. Fixit. He would even become president of something himself one day—with a little help from his friends—without knowing quite how it was done but having expected something of the sort ever since childhood. Then Mme. Levesque and Levesque *père*—by now a senior ambassador and nearing retirement—would throw a great party. Wayne would of course be invited to celebrate Bernard's well-deserved good fortune. And there on the long polished tables, surrounded by the inevitable ambassadors, ministers, minor princes and showbiz celebrities would be the inevitable *quenelles* and *tournedos* and *saltimboccas* and *crêpes* for ever and ever, amen.

Wayne stared out bitterly over the barren landscape and thought of his own parents. It was no use pretending that his mother—a chirpy matron from the South of England—was in the same class as the gracious, sophisticated and deliciously catty Mme. Levesque. As for his father, Wayne Bulkeley, Sr. was a middle-ranking executive from Baltimore in a middle-ranking American oil company whose latest enthusiasms were for good wine and Transcendental Meditation. All his father's friends and colleagues were into TM. The company (Mid-Occidental Petroleum Engineering

Corporation or MOPEC for short) now employed its own TM gurus to help its executives meditate happily when abroad, and it was by no means the only company to do so.

Wayne thought of the guru responsible for MOPEC in Zibala. He was called simply Titadhamma, a name he had taken with his Buddhist vows when he left college in America and abandoned his former self known as Phil Bayley. Titadhamma was inevitably bearded and beaded, and the guilty snarled-up MOPEC guys just loved him. They sat around in circles at his bare feet, twisting their gin-stiffened limbs into postures so painful that they would not have done it for hard cash. Wayne had once interrupted a TM session in the sitting room at home. That day his father had been playing host, and the other executives and their wives had trooped in for an evening of Titadhamma's special brand of healing. For what seemed like hours the chanting of mantras had sounded from behind the closed door, much to the unease of Ali and the other Zibalan servants, who presumably suspected heresies which Allah would not tolerate. After a while, however, silence fell, and thinking the session was over, Wayne opened the door and peeped in.

The sight of all those middle-aged men and women sitting on the floor with their legs crossed, their hands folded in their laps and their eyes closed, had been a revelation to him. Their faces had had a naked quality, he decided later, like those of sleeping babies. Ed Beckerman, his father's hearty boss, had apparently withdrawn completely into himself leaving only the tip of his tongue protruding. His wife, Cathy, who had recently recovered from a hysterectomy rolled her eyes regularly behind closed and lizard-like lids as if she were watching an inner game of tennis. Senior Vice-President Morton King, on the other hand, twitched his lips in silent prayer or possibly mental arithmetic. In front of this group sat Titadhamma, the outline of his limbs beneath his robe suggesting that he was locked into an extreme and exquisite posture. To Wayne's eyes he looked frankly asleep, a condition probably explained by Ali's mistake of having left him unattended in a room containing a drinks' cabinet earlier in the evening.

The point was, as Wayne realized at the time, his family and their friends could all too easily be mocked. His mother's obsession with providing huge quantities of very solid food had nothing to do with *haute cuisine*. His father's pretensions to getting together a wine cellar was a bid to be thought less of a hick. While the fashion for a lot of crass materialists to think themselves reborn as spiritual beings at the cost only of swollen knee joints was, Wayne knew, self-delusion of the grossest kind. By comparison the Levesque family and the diplomatic community struck him as clever, sophisticated and in touch with an altogether more serious kind of reality.

A faint shout brought Wayne out of his daydream. He leaned forward and peered over the edge. He could not see Bernard who was presumably calling impatiently from below, but he registered that the shadows cast by the four towers and the surrounding rocks had lengthened considerably. He had spent much longer than intended up here although he was still confident of getting home before dark. There should, he calculated as he squeezed his way back through the porthole into the dim space beyond, still be an hour and a half's light left. Even if they lost the track they could scarcely miss the direction home as the distant city would be ablaze with lights.

However, he did feel a bit guilty at having kept Bernard waiting at the bottom. Then he concentrated on getting down the steps in one piece, leaning into the wall and sliding the side of his body downwards in reassuring contact with the stone. He was vaguely aware of Bernard waiting for him at the bottom, but it was not until he hopped off the last step that he realized it was not Bernard at all.

The man took a pace forward, whipped out a hand and seized him crushingly by the throat. With the other hand he pushed the muzzle of a machine-gun into Wayne's yielding stomach. Wayne was paralyzed with surprise, pain and fear.

"*Aiwa!*" yelled the man. "I've got him!" The Arabic words echoed up and down the tower like the cries of ravens. There was an answering shout from the bottom of the ramp and the sound of someone coming up at a run.

The man pushed Wayne roughly back against the wall, pinning him there by the hand at his neck. Even though his own hands were free, Wayne found he could not move. All he could think of was the pain in his throat: his whole being seemed to center around it.

"*Tayyib,*" said a voice, and Wayne became aware that the man's companion had arrived. Abruptly his throat was freed, and he slumped down, half sitting and half fallen, onto the end of a window embrasure. Through involuntary tears he could see the two shapes standing in front of him.

"Now what?" asked one in Arabic.

"We wait for Tewfiq. He must have finished checking the guards by now. Tewfiq!" he yelled down the ramp. "Up here!"

Wayne, his hands at his throat, was still trying to swallow the mouthful of metallic spittle with which the assault had left him. The pain had lessened, but his throat felt crunchy as if full of crushed cartilage. Through the window a movement caught his tear-filled eyes. Far below, a blond figure leading two horses was picking its way stealthily among the fallen columns and blocks of masonry. Bernard was moving with extreme caution, and even as Wayne watched, he disappeared behind the half-dismantled wall of a mausoleum. Wayne turned back from the window just in time to see the arrival at the top of the ramp of the third man. His captors waved their guns in his direction. Tewfiq took one look at Wayne and stopped dead.

"That's not him, you fools. It's the *other* one, not this fat oaf." He stood over Wayne and grabbed a handful of the boy's hair. "Where is he?" he asked in English. "Where's your friend Levesque?"

Wayne screwed up his face against this new pain. "I don't know," he managed to gasp. Bang went his head against the stonework; his scalp seemed to tear and his cheeks felt suddenly wet. It could not have been Bernard whose shout he had heard. "Ow, shit," he moaned, sobbing, "I don't know. He went down to wait for me. He's downstairs somewhere."

His hair was released and his hands instinctively shot up.

"Right," said Tewfiq decisively in Arabic. "You come with me, Sami. Farid, you stay with this puppy. If he moves an inch, shoot his toe off, understood?"

"*Meshi*," said Farid. "No problem."

"There will be if we don't get Levesque, pea brain." Tewfiq started down the ramp at a run. "It's you who'll be held responsible."

Their footsteps and voices died away. Wayne sat on the windowsill nursing his hurt head. His throat was so painful he could barely swallow, and there was blood mixed with the tears on his face from the wound in his scalp. He stared blankly at his thighs, aware of wetness dripping onto the material from the end of his nose, trying to make some sense of what had happened. Nothing would come; his brain also seemed paralyzed by the sudden blows. All he could think was that it was all a mistake: at any moment it would all be cleared up and people would start apologizing as they usually did. The minutes dragged by, but nothing happened except that Farid suddenly stepped forward and slowly thrust the dusty black muzzle of his gun towards Wayne's mouth.

"*Musshu*," he said in Arabic. "Suck it; go on," he grinned, splitting Wayne's upper lip against a front tooth. Beyond protest, Wayne let the hard metal slide between his teeth. "Suck," commanded the man. Obediently the boy worked his dry tongue around the end of the barrel, tasting grit and oil mixed with the salt of his own blood. Despite the pain it caused his throat, Wayne was crying openly now, his slumped and passive body shaken by sobs. Farid stood in front of him, legs confidently straddled, holding his gun loosely and almost casually in one hand. Then he stepped back again.

"Dog," he said. "Son of a foreign dog. American dog." He was wearing the usual rough khaki drill of the Zibalan army, the flimsy material tacked together at the seams by large irregular stitching. The uniform bore no shoulder patches or badges of any kind. He was wearing the simple peasant's headdress of a length of white cotton material wrapped loosely around on itself, and his brown feet were bare. Following the boy's gaze, Farid looked at his own feet and then at Wayne's suede desert boots. He motioned at them with the muzzle of his gun.

"Take them off," he ordered. Wayne bent and unlaced them, kicking them off. "Now put them on me," said Farid, thrusting a foot at Wayne. The boy knelt and tried to work one of the boots onto the foot which was covered with callouses and felt as inflexible and rough as an unplaned plank of wood. Finally Farid was able to step back wearing Wayne's boots. He grinned with simple delight and wiggled the toes up and down.

"*Mazbut*," he said. "Very good."

At this moment Tewfiq called up the tower. "Bring him down," he ordered. Farid gestured Wayne to his feet and prodded him all the way down the ramp with the muzzle of the gun. Tewfiq and Sami were standing just inside the doorway.

"He's got away," said Tewfiq. "We've got the wrong dog and we've let the right one escape. We can't find the horses so he must have taken them."

"Let me go after him," said Farid eagerly. "I'll catch the bastard."

"No." Tewfiq shook his head. "This place is too big. He's got a head start and the light's going. We can't spare the time."

"Yes, let's get out of here," said a tall man Wayne had not seen before. "When Levesque gets back to al-Mazar, they'll turn the whole army out to look for us."

"So what do we do with this?" demanded Farid. "One through the neck?" he suggested, and Wayne felt his intestines squeeze with dread.

"No," said Tewfiq suddenly. Evidently he had made his mind up. "Never mind about Levesque. *Malesh.* Maybe this one will do instead. What's your name?" he asked in English. "Are you Wayne?"

"Yes," admitted Wayne, wondering how he knew.

"So maybe Mr. Wayne will do," said Tewfiq. "After all, what's the difference? Sons of foreigners, sons of dogs." He stepped through the doorway and whistled piercingly with two fingers. At once there came the sound of an engine starting up and a sand-colored vehicle with a canvas top roared out from behind a ruined archway. His captors prodded Wayne into a shambling trot with their guns and, when the vehicle screeched to a halt with pebbles popping under its heavy-treaded tires, bundled him up over the tailboard before piling in after him. From behind the mausoleum a hundred yards away an unseen Bernard watched the truck shoot forward, engine howling, and head out into the desert in a southerly direction parallel to the line of towers. The last Bernard saw of Wayne was one plump thigh still sticking up above the edge of the tailboard. Then when the noise of the engine had died away, he let go of his own horse's bridle, mounted Wayne's horse and wheeled it viciously around to face the city, digging his heels hard into its body.

Chapter 2

By SEVEN O'CLOCK that night the news of the kidnapping was widely known among the foreign community of al-Mazar, although there were various versions of the event and several different victims were confidently named. Wayne's parents were at once escorted to the American Embassy and their house put under guard. Bernard, after an epic ride which had won him the grudging admiration of several people who privately wished he had been kidnapped instead, was visited in the Quebec Embassy by a high-ranking Zibalan army officer, the Undersecretary of Security, and a plump man in a baggy suit described as the Deputy Head of Civilian Intelligence. Also present were Bernard's father and the Embassy doctor, who hovered in the background anxiously scanning Bernard for signs of imminent collapse.

At first Bernard was beautifully composed and answered the various questions succinctly and accurately. No, he had not seen the men's faces; he had not been close enough. He had seen four men with guns and had shouted a warning to Wayne when he saw one of them going into the tower. Then he heard one of them mention the name "Levesque" and realized that they were after himself as well as Wayne. He said that since he and Wayne were no match for four men armed with automatic weapons he thought the best thing he could do was hide and then go for help.

"Very sensible too," said Bernard's father. "You did exactly the right thing."

"Very sensible," echoed the Zibalan Undersecretary. "This is terrible. It is very bad for Zibala and the *détente*."

"It's not very good for Wayne, either," said Bernard with some sarcasm.

"Very bad," agreed the Undersecretary. "What will the foreign investors say? We welcome Western companies here, but they will wonder what kind of a country they are coming to where such things can happen."

"Are you sure you shouted to your friend?" broke in the army man. He looked surprisingly dapper in his beautifully-tailored uniform, his breast a multicolored riot of ribbons and awards.

"Of course I am," said Bernard. "I said so, didn't I?"

"Quite a reasonable question, Bernard," said his father with a touch of reproof.

"You see," said the army officer, "I am puzzled that they did not give chase. Surely if they heard you shouting they would have done?"

Bernard shrugged, uncrossed his legs and then recrossed them the other way. "You would have thought so. But perhaps they didn't hear me after all. Perhaps I didn't shout quite as loud as I imagined. Three of them ran out to the well, but they just ran back in again when they discovered that I had taken the horses. I was sitting tight, believe me."

"*Bien sûr*," said his father, giving him an encouraging smile.

The officer was persistent. "So from that moment they seemed to lose interest in you?"

"Who knows?" Bernard was beginning to look ruffled. "The only help I could be to Wayne was by not being caught. They seemed more concerned with getting away from Ramla as fast as possible."

"In this Land Rover?"

"Land Rover, Jeep, something of the sort. I can't recognize cars."

"No," said the officer. "I don't suppose so. And you say you didn't hear them arrive?"

"Look," said Bernard, "I'm telling you what I saw. For all I know they may have flown in by helicopter three hours earlier. What I saw was them going off in a Land Rover."

"Can you say in what direction?"

"Yes," said Bernard, "it was south. If you ask me they were heading for that *wadi* which meets up with the desert road to Tel el Aini. Once on that, they'd be able to make fast time, I should think."

"Oh," said the officer. "Where to?"

"Wherever they were going, of course," said Bernard. "How would I know?"

The army man raised an eyebrow. "Thank you," he said. "You have been most helpful. And now, Excellency," he said to Ambassador Levesque and getting briskly up, "I must leave you and help co-ordinate the search. Believe me, we are doing absolutely everything that we can."

"Everything," echoed the Undersecretary.

"But, Papa, what the hell did they expect me to do?" burst out Bernard when they had gone, leaving him with a feeling of punctured heroism. "That damned officer as good as said that I ran out on Wayne, and he even managed to imply that I was practically in the plot. *Mon Dieu, quel cochon.*"

"Don't worry," said his father, laying a hand on his shoulder. "Nobody here thinks that. If it's any consolation, I think you behaved like a true diplomat's son. Presence of mind is always what counts. Now we must wait. That officer was right about one thing: the Zibalans really will be doing all they possibly can to find him."

Three hundred yards away in the American Embassy the U.S. Ambassador was saying exactly the same words to Mr. and Mrs. Bulkeley. Wayne's mother had clearly been crying but was now making a brave effort to be calm.

"But why Wayne?" Mr. Bulkeley asked for the tenth time.

The Ambassador shrugged. "Who knows? Perhaps it's

someone needing a bit of ransom money who chose a U.S.
citizen because we have this unenviable reputation for being
rich. On the other hand they may not want money at all.
They may be political, in which case . . ." he shot a glance
at Wayne's mother and then looked enquiringly at her
husband.

"You can go on, I'm not a child," said Mrs. Bulkeley
impatiently. "This is my son you're talking about. I want to
know what the odds are. You mean if 'they' are political they
may use Wayne as some kind of pawn to bargain with?"

"Exactly," said the Ambassador gratefully. "That's very
realistic of you, Mrs. Bulkeley. I'm afraid that is what I had in
mind."

"Well, who are 'they'?" asked Wayne's father.

"Quite honestly, I know no more than you do. I have had
the President of Zibala himself on the telephone not ten
minutes before you came in and he asked the same question.
But until we hear from the kidnappers we can't be sure of
anything." He looked helplessly from one parent to the other
and then brightened as a thought struck him. "Can I freshen
up your drinks?"

Presently the phone rang and the Ambassador said
"Speaking, Mr. President." He listened intently for a while
and then replaced the receiver. "Well," he said, "that was the
President. Theirs, not ours," he added unnecessarily,
misinterpreting the hopeful look on Mrs. Bulkeley's face.
"Ismail Barzuq. Uh, he says the army is out there at Ramla
searching the whole place at this moment. They haven't
found anything yet, and until there's a message from the
kidnappers, the President says he's not allowing the news
media even to report Wayne's disappearance. Frankly, he
didn't sound too hopeful about finding your boy tonight.
This was obviously a planned operation, and it's impossible
to search the desert in darkness. The Zibalan air force is
sending up reconnaissance aircraft at first light, though.
Damn," he said with feeling, "what kind of bastards would

do a thing like this?" He passed a hand wearily over his neat and greying hair.

The Bulkeleys stayed that night at the U.S. Embassy. It was agreed that they would be far safer there and in any case they wanted to be the first to hear if any news of Wayne came in. The night dragged on, but nobody slept. An uneasy tension reigned in which doors were opened very softly to admit the bearers of many cups of coffee and people walked about the corridors with unnatural quietness. The Ambassador chain-smoked and blocked incoming calls from his wife in the Residence who wanted him to come to bed. Mr. Bulkeley stared at the telephone. Wayne's mother sat rather calmly and smiled reassuringly at the Embassy doctor when pressed to accept a great variety of pills. "I'm perfectly all right, thank you," was all she said. "I just hope they feed Wayne properly, that's all."

After a bit Titadhamma arrived. Quite early on, it had been suggested that he should be called, but owing to al-Mazar's hopeless telephone system the Embassy switchboard had wasted time trying to get through. Eventually someone had been dispatched to fetch him. He arrived looking very dignified in a robe, like a priest called to a bedside, disseminating an aura of philosophic calm and a faint scent of patchouli. He and Mr. Bulkeley went off to meditate in an empty office with a request that they should not be disturbed.

"Supposing a call comes through?" asked Wayne's mother, who had declined an invitation to join them. The guru looked at the telephone with a half-smile.

"I am afraid the phone will not ring," he announced, and much to everyone's surprise it didn't.

A mile and a half away ten Zibalan soldiers were guarding the Bulkeleys' darkened villa. Over the road and partly concealed by a bougainvillea hedge was parked a truck belonging to Internal Security. It, too, had its lights off. Inside the compartment at the back was a good deal of radio equipment and a tiny steel table around which three men were sitting in their shirt sleeves playing cards. A few lights winked and glowed on a panel screwed to the forward bulkhead, and the compartment was full of the soft rushing noise of a radio turned to a carrier wave. Periodically a harsh message would interrupt and the men would look up from their game. But they would always go back to it, sweat pouring down their faces as their incessant smoking raised the temperature in their stuffy metal cell.

Chapter 3

FOR THE FIRST twenty minutes his captors ignored Wayne as the Land Rover roared along. He had eventually pulled himself up from the floor and onto one of the two bare steel benches which stretched down each side of the vehicle. At first they had kept the setting sun on their right, and they soon reached the dried-up *wadi* which Wayne recognized from a long trek he and Bernard had once made down the riverbed on horseback. To his surprise they bounced along it for a mile or two in the direction away from the road which led to the south of Zibala by way of the desert villages. Then they changed direction again and were now heading westwards into the wilderness, the sun a great orange ball above the horizon ahead. The driver, whose neck Wayne noticed irrelevantly was covered with the scars of many boils, concentrated on avoiding the worst of the cracks and crevices in the baked and stony ground they were crossing. This kind of terrain extended, Wayne knew, for about three hundred miles. It was as much true desert as the endless dunes of the great sand seas beyond and to the south: a trackless plateau of loose shale, exposed rock and patches of dried brush which, one spring out of every half dozen, turned green and bloomed all in a month before the light rain stopped and they were again reduced to clumps of parched twigs.

Across this the Land Rover jolted and bounced. Wayne could see the speedometer needle swinging to cover the 50 mark, the low-geared engine roaring and the hard suspension often kicking the rear wheels into the air. Tewfiq sat in front on the driver's right, grasping the metal grab handle bolted to the doorframe. Sami, Farid and the tall man, whose name was Ibrahim, held on to the hoops which supported the canvas awning covering the back, often being left hanging briefly in midair before slamming back onto the bench. Each time the vehicle left the ground, it came down again with a great crash, jets of dust puffing up through the gaps between the steel plates of the floor. The men each used one hand to hold their guns across their laps to cushion the blows, but very often muzzle smashed against stock and once a spare clutch of full magazines cascaded to the floor.

No call was made for the driver to slacken speed. Wayne wondered how soon they expected pursuit. He tried to estimate how long it would take Bernard to get back to the stables and raise the alarm—always assuming that the telephones between Assuf and the city center were working. There again, he might have a fall or the horse break a leg. Miserably Wayne realized that there was no hope of any organized search before nightfall—which meant nothing would happen before dawn the following day. By which time . . . he blotted out the rest of that thought before his mind could suggest the horrid alternatives of his fate.

Now and again Tewfiq would raise his left hand and silently indicate a course correction to the driver, and Wayne could see he held a compass in his fist. Farid must suddenly have noticed the boy's curiosity for with a backhand blow of his weapon he knocked Wayne back into his seat, following up with a crack across the kneecaps from the gun's skeleton stock. Wayne crouched over in agony, eyes blurring with tears once more. The Land Rover leaped like a shying horse, and his nose smashed forward into his own knee and began bleeding.

After a bit Tewfiq shouted something above the noise of the engine, and the driver nodded. He swung the wheel, and they headed towards a low sandstone cliff which rose abruptly to their left. He brought them to a halt in the lee of the cliff and switched off the engine. For a moment nobody moved, as if collecting battered wits. A stinging silence fell, and gas could be heard sloshing in the vehicle's tank. Then Tewfiq sprang out and shouted an order. Ibrahim leaned over and released a catch. The back of the passenger seat hinged forward revealing what looked to Wayne like a powerful but compact radio set. He was beginning to be past caring.

Nevertheless he listened as the men busied themselves, their voices urgent. For the first time he was really grateful that he had picked up more than a smattering of Arabic. None of his schoolmates had made the least effort to acquaint themselves with a language which, by common consent of the foreign community, was a barbaric tongue of no earthly use to man or beast. While his friends had been sunning themselves around the pool at the Sporting Club, he had mooned about at home chatting to Ali the servant, or had roamed off alone to the Old Quarter of al-Mazar.

He had never told his parents that he had crossed the invisible *cordon sanitaire* which separated the white Western community from the seething Eastern city in which they had temporarily wound up. Expatriates stuck together, Wayne had long ago discovered. They formed little groups among themselves according to nationality, profession or hobby. They ran the Italian Cultural Center or the Ramla Ladies' Club; they played golf together or joined Transcendental Meditation sessions. But over and above those minor groupings the foreign community made a large group on its own whose children mostly went to the American School and who saw al-Mazar and Zibala as yet another staging place, one more posting on a salaried pilgrimage around the world. The men were sent by their companies, by their corporations, by their banks, by their diplomatic services. They came and dug for oil, or taught Zibalans how to use lathes, or installed sophisticated aids for brain surgery in al-Mazar's only teaching hospital. And their families trailed after them, sat out the tour of duty in a rented air-conditioned villa, played a lot of bridge, drank a lot of scotch, and left for somewhere else. Wayne knew that practically none of these international nomads—his own parents included—had any real interest in the countries and cultures they visited. To them Zibala was just one more sweat hole, and Arabic one more language fit only for servants.

Wayne's sneaked hours in the *souks* of al-Mazar constituted the most independent act of his entire life. He had started visiting the *souks* when he was fourteen, terrified but curious, on each occasion edging a few alleys further into the center of the Old City. Dreadful tales circulated among the foreign community which told of the Zibalans' unspeakable cruelty, their unpredictable outbursts of violence, their lying, thieving and general untrustworthiness. It was even rumored darkly that they still indulged their centuries-old tradition of slaving, while unmentionable things were certain to happen to any fair-skinned lad who fell into their clutches.

Yet each time Wayne ventured timorously into the *souks* and nothing happened he gained a little confidence. He saw much which bewildered and horrified him; he was upset by what he could only see as the Zibalans' wanton cruelty to their animals and their apparent indifference to their own suffering. Yet as he himself was shown only considerable kindness and warmth he felt able to overlook this. True to their religious traditions of hospitality, the Arabs of Zibala were in fact rather well disposed towards foreigners. Periodically a political upheaval occurred when the country indulged in an orgy of antiforeign feeling: a few offices were set on fire, the American School was temporarily closed down and its teachers stoned. But always the cloud passed, and the Zibalans—as if immediately forgetful of their lapse—went back to being their usual easy-going selves.

Wayne had made friends with a family who kept a scents and essences stall in the inner *souk* and was made to feel an honored guest whenever he came. He was, he knew, a source of considerable pride to the family for his presence aroused great interest in the alley. Children would come from all directions to greet him, watch him wide-eyed and stroke his clothes. So it was that Wayne's first attempts to communicate with them in their own language were welcomed with cries of amazement and encouragement.

This was a part of his life which he kept a secret. He was much worried that Bernard might find out. He felt obscurely guilty, as if by such a deliberate act of "slumming" he had betrayed all that Bernard stood for and everything to which he himself aspired. Nevertheless he kept going, defiantly, and his knowledge of Arabic slowly improved.

The tailboard of the Land Rover was released with a crash and Wayne was pulled out, falling heavily onto the stony ground. Farid prodded him to his feet with his gun muzzle and guided him away from the vehicle until he was standing some twenty yards away with his back to the cliff. They surely can't be going to shoot me here and now, he thought with a clench of fear. What was the point of bringing me all this way in the first place? They could have done it on the spot at Ramla.

"What are you going to do?" he asked Farid in Arabic but the man gave no sign of having heard the question. Suddenly Wayne was overcome with a desperate need to urinate. They can't very well shoot me for that, he told himself. He turned and peed against the cliff. When he had finished, he found that Farid had been watching him with a half-smile of amusement. Then the man hawked and spat and looked over his shoulder to see how his companions were getting on.

The men were grouped around a Morse key which Tewfiq

had set up on the hood of the Land Rover. He was sending a message, Wayne decided, although the man was pressing the key so slowly, reading the groups off a sheet of paper Ibrahim held, that he might almost have been practicing. He was clearly not a trained radio operator. Tewfiq finished, and they began dismantling the equipment. Wayne looked about him.

The sun was half below the horizon, and the whole landscape was suffused with a deep red glow. The sandstone cliffs burned, the desert stretched away on all sides in various shades of gold and orange. In the distance—Wayne estimated about twenty-five miles away—the towers of Ramla caught the last rays of the sun like four little bronze pegs hammered into the horizon. Even as he watched, they seemed to float as the shadow cast by the earth's curvature crept up them until only the four domes caught the light. Then they too winked out and became invisible against the deepening purple sky. He shuddered, immensely alone.

He turned his head to see Tewfiq coming over. The man said something to Farid who went back to join his companions, busy filling the Land Rover's fuel tank from jerry cans carried in racks above the front bumper. Tewfiq stood for a moment looking reflectively at Wayne before he spoke. The boy realized later that he must indeed have been a sorry sight: his face and trousers smeared with blood, his lip swollen, one side of his head matted, standing numbly there in the desert in stockinged feet.

"I have just sent a message," said Tewfiq in fluent English. "Our organization has been informed that it is you we have and not Levesque. It will make an announcement immediately to the press and radio. The announcement will say simply that you have been taken into custody and will be held until our imprisoned comrades here in Zibala have been released and flown to a neutral country. Then you will be free to go."

"You . . . you're not the army?"

Tewfiq laughed without evident amusement. "No," he said, "we're not the army."

"Then who are you?"

"Our organization is called the Seventh January. Have you ever heard of it?"

"I think so," said Wayne, anxious not to offend.

"You will become very familiar with us," Tewfiq told him. "So will the whole world. By breakfast time tomorrow you and we will all be famous."

"But how long . . ." began Wayne, "I mean, supposing they don't free these friends of yours. What happens then?"

"You will be executed," said Tewfiq, "as they will. They are under sentence of death. Not that their deaths could be avenged if you were to die a thousand times. But you will die once—this we have sworn."

Wayne felt his knees go fluid. "You can't just kill someone in cold blood," he protested. Tewfiq did not even deign to reply.

"How old are you?" he asked Wayne.

"Fifteen. Fifteen and a half."

"Then you are not a child any longer. You are a man. You can die like one if necessary."

"In my own country I wouldn't be allowed to fight in a war until I was eighteen. And even the death sentence has practically been abolished."

"But you are not in your own country," said Tewfiq unanswerably. "You are in Zibala. Here you are a man."

"How is it you speak English so well?" Wayne asked as if to undermine the cold implacability of Tewfiq's tone with a personal question.

"I was at university," explained the Arab with an unmistakable touch of pride. "In England, at a place called Sussex. Most of the world will speak English one day, so if you want to get anywhere you just have to learn it, like it or not. I don't very much. Now let's go," he said, dismissing the subject as if it bored him.

"Where to?" asked Wayne. He was forced into the Land

Rover once more and the driver started the engine. They drove in the deepening twilight out across the desert on a course which Tewfiq plotted with the aid of his compass. He often checked his watch, too. Wayne presumed he was navigating by some sort of dead reckoning in this wilderness without maps. Nobody spoke. The hectic jolting and bouncing was less now because the light was too bad for speed. Since Tewfiq would not allow the headlights to be switched on, the driver had to manage with the curious afterglow of sunset which the desert seemed to retain for a while like the heat of the day. The hours passed.

Just before ten o'clock Tewfiq once again gave the order to halt. They climbed out and the radio was switched on. After a moment the distorted strains of "Lilliburlero" were heard followed by six pips.

"Nineteen hours, Greenwich Mean Time," came the announcer's voice. "BBC World Service. The News, read by Graham Sandilands.

"We have just heard that a group of rebels in the Middle Eastern state of Zibala today kidnapped the son of an American oil company executive. The rebels are demanding the release of five political prisoners in exchange for the boy's life. The major bush fires which have been threatening the Australian town of . . ."

"These are just the headlines," Tewfiq explained to his men in Arabic. They had clearly understood little of what the announcer was saying. "It's number one in the news, anyway. Sh!" He raised a warning hand. "It's coming on again."

"Reports coming in from al-Mazar in the last half hour say that a group of rebels have kidnapped the fifteen-year-old son of a MOPEC executive in Zibala. The boy, Wayne Bulkeley, was taken when he and a friend were out riding together. His friend managed to get away, but the executive's son was driven off into the desert. A massive search has been launched for him.

"The rebels, who call themselves the Seventh January, say

they will release the boy unharmed when five other
members of their group, currently under sentence of death
in Zibala, are flown to a neutral country. The Seventh
January are believed to be a purely Zibalan organization
although loosely affiliated to the Palestine Liberation
Organization. The group gained prominence in September
last year when it claimed responsibility for blowing up a
plane on an internal flight in Zibala, killing the Zibalan
Foreign Minister Mr. Mamduh Fanous and three French
schoolteachers.

"The Zibalan authorities say that a massive search
operation for the boy has been mounted by the army and air
force. The five men whose release is being demanded by the
terrorists are awaiting execution for acts of sabotage during
the recent wave of unrest which accompanied the General
Election in Zibala."

The announcer coughed slightly and changed gear. "This
news comes to you in the World Service of the BBC. The ten-
day-old bush fires which have been raging uncontrollably in
the Australian State of Qu . . ." Tewfiq cut the voice off
abruptly.

"*Yallah,*" he said softly to the driver. "Let's go."

On they drove until by Wayne's watch it was twenty to
one. Nobody spoke except for an occasional murmured
direction from Tewfiq. They ground on across the desert
without even sidelights, but Wayne realized that this was less
to avoid being seen than to prevent the driver's vision being
spoiled by the dashboard lights. There was no moon but the
sky was liberally sprinkled with stars so bright that the Land
Rover cast a faint shadow directly underneath. It was
bitterly cold. Wayne tried to doze but was continually jolted
out of sleep by ruts or the ache in his nearly bare feet. The
nylon socks he wore offered no warmth, and the cold had
long ago reduced his feet to almost numb blocks with only
enough feeling left to transmit a steady pain.

In that semi-conscious state which comes from tiredness

and nervous exhaustion Wayne's mind drifted among the day's events like sand among ancient monuments. None of what had happened to him seemed real any longer. The overdose of reality he had sustained had had the effect of making events cloudy and dreamlike. Twenty-four hours ago I was safely at home in bed, he thought. He imagined the quiet ticking of the luminous alarm clock on his bedside table. It would still be going even if nobody had wound it because it went for eight days. It would still be going somewhere hundreds of miles away, just the same as ever. Except now he was not in bed; he was under sentence of death in a vehicle lost in the middle of a wilderness . . . His parents floated in and out of his fitful doze. Soon they would be coming down to breakfast without him, Ali bringing in his father's bacon and eggs, undeterred by having to cook pork. "Good Moslems make the best servants." Who was it he had heard say that? Bernard? His mother? True, his mother had experience of a wide range of servants. Before coming to the Middle East, they had lived in Brunei where all the servants had been Chinese, and in Venezuela where they had been Catholics . . . On furlough in America his mother had been quite lost without her servants. It was something she had grown accustomed to, something almost unknown now in the developed countries except as the privilege of the very rich. His poor mother. Wayne's closed eyes oozed tears of self-pity.

He awoke with a start, suddenly aware that the Land Rover had halted again. The back slammed down and the canvas flap was pulled aside.

"Get out," said Tewfiq.

Wayne climbed stiffly down. As soon as he straightened up, the light desert wind cut through his thin clothes, searching out and evaporating all the little crevices and pockets of heat trapped by the sitting position he had been in. Dumbly he looked at his watch and shivered. Almost half past two. They must have come miles. He stood miserably with shoulders hunched, his hands in his pockets, conscious only of the cold, the blank starlight and the sharp stones underfoot.

In the back of the Land Rover two of the men had set up a Primus stove. Its soft roar seemed to fill the desert. After a long wait Tewfiq came up carrying a tin mug.

"Drink," he said, thrusting it at Wayne. Gratefully the boy cupped the scalding metal in his hands, letting the heat seep into his palms. He took a sip. Black tea made so strong that even the usual Zibalan overdose of sugar could not disguise the bitterness of tannin. Sensation began returning although his feet remained blocks of ice. His split lip stung to the hot liquid, his bruised throat ached to the swallowing. Then the men were emptying the teapot and the dregs from their mugs onto the ground, stowing the Primus and getting ready to move.

"How much longer?" Wayne asked as Tewfiq motioned him in.

"Who knows?" said the man.

"No, I mean now. How much further have we to go?"

"An hour or two," said Tewfiq vaguely. "Soon."

"When does it get light?"

"Questions, questions. About six. They will start the search then." Tewfiq spat generously. "Don't pretend to yourself they will find us. They haven't a hope. Those soldiers couldn't find a camel on a soccer field. Soldiers!" He spat once more. "Sons of dogs, stupid as lumps of dung."

They resumed their journey. In a few minutes Wayne found himself hunching back into his old position, and after a quarter of an hour the brief warmth produced by the cup of tea had ebbed away again leaving him as cold as before. Only now he found he could not doze: the only legacy of the tea was to keep him awake.

For the first time he thought seriously about his chances of escaping. His mind invented and rejected mad scenarios, beginning with somehow easing himself unnoticed over the back of the vehicle and running away into the desert to be spotted at dawn by a conveniently passing helicopter. His reason did not even bother to point out the futility of such a plan. Alternatively, he might make a lunge, grab one of the guns, force the vehicle to stop and make the men run off with their hands above their heads while he drove away. But it would not be quite like that, Wayne admitted miserably to himself. In the first place he utterly lacked the nerve ever to make such a move. Moreover, he was not at all sure he knew how to make one of these guns work, and he was absolutely certain he would stall the Land Rover the first time he tried to drive it. Ideas of escape would clearly have to wait; he must take his chance when offered it and not before.

It was just after five o'clock when the Land Rover, which had been climbing for some time, came to a halt.

"That's it," said Tewfiq in Arabic. "Everybody out. Let's get this thing hidden."

Wayne found that they had arrived in what seemed to be mountainous country. On all sides the horizon was formed by jagged lines of rock which blotted out all except the stars directly overhead.

Tewfiq was giving staccato orders. "Ibrahim, get the radio and the spare batteries. Farid, the water. Sami, the guns. Adil, the food."

"There isn't any food," said Adil the driver. "We left it too late; I couldn't get any safely."

"No food at all?"

"Nothing. Tea and sugar only."

"Bring them. Also the stove and the mugs."

The equipment was unloaded and two large jerry cans of water were unstrapped from their racks. When the Land Rover was empty, Tewfiq started it up and drove it away behind some rocks, leaving the group standing in a huddle as if suddenly paralyzed. After a minute the distant sound of the engine stopped and Tewfiq reappeared.

"They won't find that," he asserted confidently. "On this

ground we've not left so much as a tire mark between here
and Ramla. They won't know where to begin." He glanced
at his watch, angling it up to catch the starlight. "Half an
hour, to be safe," he said. "Let's get a move on. Anyone got a
flashlight?" Two of the men answered. "No lights, okay?"
ordered Tewfiq. "You, Farid, keep an eye on Fatty there."
He set off and the others picked up their burdens and
followed. Farid took up the jerry cans of water and then
dropped one of them again. He kicked it with his newly-
acquired footwear.

"Bring it," he said. "You won't run far carrying that."

Wayne picked up the can. The weight was unbelievable,
the metal handle dragging on his frozen hand. He began
picking his way slowly after the others, stumbling and
gasping when his feet came down heavily on sharp-edged
stones or stubbed against protruding rocks. Farid punched
him coaxingly in the back.

"Come on," he said, "faster. You heard Tewfiq; time's
short."

Wayne plodded on, whimpering, lugging the unbalancing
dead weight which banged against his legs and grazed the
ground if he let himself stoop at all. Most of his brain could
think of nothing but the pain and the necessity to endure it,
but a delirious fraction played feverishly with little sums.
The jerry can probably held twenty-five liters: Say thirty
kilos including a bit for the can itself. Surely thirty kilos could
not be this heavy? He dropped the can to change hands, but
not before his own boot on Farid's foot had caught his ankle
a painful kick.

"Get on, get on. I know old women who are stronger than
you. What are you waiting for, a servant?" Farid added
sneeringly. His own jerry can dangled from one meaty fist.

Wearily, Wayne bent and took a fresh grip. Both hands
were so sore he could scarcely remember which one was due
for a rest. He vaguely knew that up ahead the others had
stopped and were waiting for him to catch up. When

eventually he had lugged the can up to them, Tewfiq said impatiently:

"Take it, Farid, he's slowing us down."

Wayne dropped the can gratefully and leaned against a rock but he had scarcely drawn a breath before Tewfiq lashed out and gripped a handful of hair, yanking him upright. Wayne felt his scabbed wound tear open again and yelled with the blinding pain.

"Shut up," said Tewfiq shortly. "You'll keep up with me from now on. You're slowing us up, American puppy. It's like dragging around a sack of boiled noodles."

Suddenly the pain and insults were too much. "Screw you!" shouted Wayne. "Why do you have to keep hitting me all the time? Aren't you even civilized? I'm not one of your damn donkeys, you know. I'm not one of your ignorant peasants who don't know any bet . . ." Tewfiq's fist smashing into his mouth stopped the rest of his outburst. The boy dropped to the ground. He knelt there on all fours, shaking his head slowly like a stunned ox, waiting for the lights in front of his eyes to fade. He let blood and saliva dribble from his hanging mouth.

"You will never say that again," announced Tewfiq calmly. It was a statement, not a threat. "Just remember that whatever we do to you it will not be a fraction of what they do night and day to our comrades in prison. Now get up." He hauled Wayne to his feet by his shirt collar and prodded him gently before him.

For the next ten minutes Wayne stumbled on in silence, only occasionally gasping as his foot came down on some particularly agonizing blade of stone. Tewfiq chose the path with complete assurance, winding in and out of bulks of rock, sometimes scrambling up inclines which forced Wayne to use his hands to help himself. He wondered how Farid was managing at the back with the two jerry cans and hoped he was having a hard time. Then they halted.

"We go down here," Tewfiq explained to him. "You go

first with a flashlight, Adil. Use it only when you're inside."
Adil squeezed past them and vanished. Suddenly a glow
appeared from underground. A narrow triangular crack lit
up, framing the dark figure of Adil. They followed him at a
sharp downward angle, and from the change in the sound of
their footsteps Wayne realized they were in a cave of sorts.
Another light went on at the rear of the party so that the walls
on either side glittered with mineral facets but the ground
underfoot was still lost in darkness. They made several sharp
turns; the walls receded on either side.

"Okay," said Tewfiq. "Ibrahim and I will take a look. Give
me my gun, Sami." He took one of the flashlights and
disappeared. In thirty seconds they were back. "All clear.
About another quarter of an hour until dawn. We'll leave the
puppy here."

Wayne was too tired to feel any further menace. If he was
going to be left buried underground, they might as well put a
bullet through his head. He was utterly finished physically.
In response to the pressure of Tewfiq's hand he sank down
onto the ground and found himself sitting on soft dry sand. A
wave of weariness engulfed him and he toppled over. The
voices and the lights receded. His consciousness dwindled
to a speck and winked out.

He awoke to a sharp pain in his leg. He opened his eyes and
found Tewfiq standing over him, foot raised for another
kick.

"Wake up, dog," he said. "They're looking for you."

Wayne sat up with a sudden stab of excited hope. He got
painfully to his feet, wincing as he put his weight on them,
and limped yawningly after Tewfiq. The cave he had slept
in, he now saw, was in reality more of a passageway. From
somewhere around a bend ahead came daylight, and as he
rounded it, he blinked with surprise.

He was in one corner of a large sandstone cavern, the roof
of which was black with the soot deposits of cooking fires.

Both the floor and the ceiling sloped at the identical acute angle and were nearly smooth: it was as if the cave were simply a pocket in a regular seam of sandstone between layers of a different rock. It was a rough rectangle whose longer side he was now facing. It stretched perhaps thirty yards away to his left. What took his attention, though, was the long overhung slit like a horizontal window at ground level running the full width of the cave and admitting a brilliant gash of sunlight. Wayne could see the other men lying flat on their bellies staring out through the hole, stubble dark on their unshaven faces.

Tewfiq grasped Wayne's shirt collar. "Not too close," he warned. "We don't want you spotted." By the pressure of his arm he indicated to Wayne that he should get down and crawl forward to the slit. Wayne did so, sliding on his stomach until he came up level with Adil. Tewfiq himself lay full length on Wayne's right, still with the boy's collar tightly bunched in his fist. On belly and elbows Wayne inched forward until restrained.

"Far enough," Tewfiq said.

Wayne screwed up his eyes in the brilliant light. The view was stupendous. It was as if he were lying in some eagle's nest on a cliff face hundreds of feet above the desert floor. By turning his head he could see the same cliff extending away on either side, indented with coves and bays and sudden promontories like an inland coastline. The rocks were layered with different colored strata, worn by centuries of wind and heat to the dull ochres and reds of cooling metal. Straight ahead lay the open desert, flat as a mat to the horizon which Wayne thought might be sixty miles away. It was entirely featureless except for a sizable oasis in the left foreground. From this height and distance the oasis seemed clearly delineated as if the water under the soil were contained in a gigantic cupped hand. The dark green sponge of the palms did not fray at the edges into scattered clumps of more and more stunted trees; it ended abruptly as if trimmed off with a knife. The line where desert became oasis was no thicker than the bole of a single palm.

Amongst the trees Wayne could see the gleam of houses and in one place the single white tooth of a minaret marked a small mosque. There was no visible track leading to the oasis: it was a desert island apparently unvisited and unrelinquished, a community cut off in time and place. On closer inspection Wayne noticed that its bounds were not completely marked by palms: in one patch the trees had been cleared and irrigated and the plots of land planted. Here the vegetation was a lighter, fresher green, like that almost of ripe lettuce.

Tewfiq shook his collar gently. "You see?" he said, jerking his head to one side. "Up there. Two of them. Stupid bastards."

For a moment Wayne had no idea what he meant. Then, adjusting his eyes against the glare he looked upwards. Flying across the brilliant blue of the sky were two twin-engined aircraft. They were floating only very slightly higher than Wayne himself and not much more than three-quarters of a mile away. Then the sound of their engines reached him and he felt a pang of excitement at their nearness.

"Forget it," said Tewfiq, who must have known what Wayne was feeling. "They can't see us. There's too much overhang and we're in shadow. They can fly up and down these cliffs all day for all the good it'll do them."

"But they'll see the cave," said Wayne confidently. "Probably the pilots are reporting it on their radios at this moment."

Tewfiq laughed. "Sure they'll see it," he said, "along with all the rest. Look," he pointed.

Wayne craned his neck. Now that his eyes were used to the light he saw at once what he was expected to see and what he had missed earlier. Everywhere the sandstone strata were honeycombed with cave openings. Little round holes, ovals, slits, gashes and gaping caverns, they pocked the rock face in both directions for as far as the eye could reach. The whole exposed cliff was riddled with caves.

"There must be thousands," said Wayne faintly.

"At least. You're not going to tell me they can search all of them. They'd need an army."

"They've *got* an army. You heard what the radio said."

Tewfiq laughed again. "I doubt if the Zibalan army can produce more than fifty men with proper rock-climbing training, much less the equipment," he said. "It wouldn't be a question of sending up a lot of kids in uniform to pretend they're bird-nesting. Very few people except those who live in Bir Huzun—" he nodded downwards at the oasis "—know their way to more than a dozen of these caves. Thousands of years ago people used to live in them to escape the raids of foreign armies. Then all this desert was green. Now there is nothing and nobody comes here. Why should they? Nothing lives here but snakes and scorpions and eagles. And Seventh January," he added with a touch of pride.

The planes droned on out of sight, sunlight glinting on their metal wings.

"We will see what they are saying," said Tewfiq. "Here, Ibrahim, bring the radio over." He switched it on, trying different wavelengths while nothing but the crackle of static and faint snatches of Arab music came from the loudspeaker.

"Can't find them," he said at last. "Never mind. Soon time for the news."

When it came, the BBC could add very little to what it had said the previous night. The Zibalan Prime Minister claimed that the troops were following up a firm lead and that various arrests had been made already among known Left-wing sympathizers of the guerrilla group. Meanwhile the Zibalan Government was standing firm in its determination not to accede to the demands of terrorists and had no intention of releasing the prisoners who were convicted common criminals and not, as Seventh January described them, "political detainees." Tewfiq looked grave as he switched off.

"I wonder who they've got?" he said to the others when he had translated for them.

"Probably nobody at all," said Ibrahim. "It's just a bluff."

" 'Various arrests,' he said," muttered Adil angrily. "We all know what that means. They'll have rounded up the usual bunch of school kids and students and beaten them to a jelly. Poor devils."

"It's all they know how to do," said Tewfiq. "Not like that in your country, eh?" He shook the collar he still held in one hand as if Wayne had been the puppy he accused him of being. "Or is it?"

"Our cops sometimes arrest students," retorted Wayne. "Of course they do, if they suspect they know about something criminal. If these people who have been arrested today have no connection with any of you, the cops will just let them go."

"Stupid dog," Adil turned angrily away. He alone of the other guerrillas seemed to have some English.

"When our police take anyone in for questioning," explained Tewfiq, "they beat them first, regardless. It doesn't matter if they turn out to be innocent or guilty. You go into a police station and you get beaten. That's the way. It has always been like that. They beat you on the soles of the feet with canes until you can't walk, and then they throw you into a cell full of flies and shit to think about things."

"Our cops are not like that," said Wayne, with perhaps a fraction more firmness than he felt. He lowered his eyes against the increasing dazzle of the sunlight outside. "I'm very thirsty," he said. "Can I have some water?"

"It's rationed," said Tewfiq shortly. "It's only for drinking. If you have your share now, you can't have any tea when we make it. It's your choice."

"I'll have it now." Wayne was given a cup of water. When he had drunk it greedily he said: "Couldn't I just have a bit to wash my face?"

"Certainly," said Tewfiq with heavy sarcasm. "You're in the Hilton now. Ring for room service." His eyes travelled over the boy's face taking in the hair matted with dried blood, the puffed and swollen mouth with its split lips, the dried crust of blood and dirt smeared around his nose. "Sure," he said, "you can wash. You can use your next mug of drinking water." He poured out another ration and held it out. Miserably blinking back tears, Wayne shook his head. With a shrug Tewfiq poured it carefully back into the jerry can.

The day wore on; the sun passed its zenith. The men sat and cleaned their guns and chatted. Now and again they brewed a pot of tea. Every hour Tewfiq listened to the news, both to the BBC and to Radio Zibala, but there were no new developments except that the reports suggested the search was concentrated on the south of the country. This might mean that the authorities had fallen for Tewfiq's simple trick of setting off in the wrong direction; on the other hand, they might have wanted the group to think that.

Gradually the men talked less among themselves, and Wayne, sitting where he had been ordered at the back of the cave, thought he knew why. Clearly, everyone was becoming obsessed by the lack of food. He himself had been conscious of his empty stomach for some time: it was, after all, more than twenty-four hours since he had last eaten. Sooner or later they would be forced out into the open.

"How much longer are we going to stay here?" he asked Tewfiq.

"As long as necessary," came the short reply. "We're in no hurry."

"I'm hungry," stated Wayne. Tewfiq favored him with a long and withering look which rested momentarily on the bulge of Wayne's stomach behind his dirty shirt but said nothing. Wayne subsided.

When this is over, he told himself, I shall be treated like a hero. I shall be offered absolutely anything I want to eat. I shall be able to go into the most expensive restaurant in al-

Mazar and order whatever I want and no one will mind. I shall go to that place Bernard's always being taken to, La Pipistrelle or whatever it's called, and start right off with some huge juicy prawns . . . He began planning menus in his head, but it was a listless pastime and his interest soon flagged. His head ached and his feet throbbed. He wished he could show these people that there was no need to be so brutal all the time. He was, like characters in books he had read, simply a victim of circumstances. Yet often when he looked up he caught one or other of the men scowling at him as if he inspired personal hatred. He could not understand it.

Imperceptibly he became aware of a topic of conversation which cropped up more and more often as the men sat and waited in the mouth of the cave. He could not always follow all the rapid Arabic, but the gist seemed clear enough. Farid and Adil were arguing that he should be killed as soon as possible, and the others were opposing this idea.

"Look," Farid said finally, "we got the wrong guy, okay? It was nobody's fault . . ." here Tewfiq spat ". . . but even if it was it doesn't matter now. As far as Daoud Hafez is concerned we've botched it up. I don't think you're right about this little dog." He jerked a thumb back in Wayne's direction. "I don't think anybody gives a damn about him. Levesque was a different matter, though. His father is an ambassador, and you don't steal ambassadors' children without there being a real fuss. Old man Levesque could have brought all sorts of pressure to bear on President Barzuq: he could have threatened to cut off Québécois' aid to Zibala; he could have expelled all our diplomats from Quebec. Damn it, he could have got people to stand up in the Security Council of the UN and say that the Zibalan Government was shown to be so weak they were upsetting the balance of power in the Middle East. What do you think a rabbit like Barzuq would have done? He'd have freed the comrades like a shot and flown the lot of us out of the country, First Class if we'd asked for it. We could have dumped the Levesque boy once we'd landed and this whole operation would be over. Instead of that, what do we have? Some Yankee oilman's kid nobody cares about."

"So what do you suggest?" Tewfiq asked him.

"Farid's right," broke in Adil the driver. He had been listening, hands clasped around his knees, nodding vigorously as his friend had been speaking. "Barzuq's going to let us sweat. He's not afraid of a single American oil company kicking up a noise for a fortnight because he knows they want to hang on to their concessions in Zibala. Nobody will do anything. Sooner or later we'll have to come out and then they'll hang the lot of us as well as the comrades. I say get rid of this puppy now and let's go home. They'll never find the body here so we won't be connected. Let's face it, it's a washout; we might as well abort the mission and live to do it again properly." He looked around at his companions. Only Farid looked in agreement; Sami and Ibrahim were clearly doubtful and seemed to be watching Tewfiq for a lead. Tewfiq spat again and regarded them all with some contempt.

"All this talk of going home or flying out of the country," he said. "Have you forgotten why we have done this? It is to get the comrades released before Barzuq kills them, not to gaurantee ourselves safe passage out of the country so we can spend our lives in exile in Libya or somewhere. What are we, then—little girls that when we don't get what we want by the time our stomachs are empty we cry for our mothers and give up?" The dark eyes were angry. Farid and Adil glared at the ground.

"We all agreed to this plan. Daoud Hafez himself approved it. It is a pity that we did not get Levesque but it's not vital. You think the Americans will just say 'Too bad' and decide that this boy is expendable? Oh, yes, they might *think* it, but they'd never act as though they did. Why? Because they would be cutting their own throats. Quite apart from their Senators getting up in Congress and demanding how many American children are worth one oil concession, think of the effect it would have on all the other foreign companies in Zibala. They'd take one look and say that Zibala was too dangerous and unstable to risk any more investment, and Barzuq couldn't afford that. It's only foreign money that keeps him in power anyway, as we all know."

The men looked at each other and then back at Tewfiq.

"So," Tewfiq said, "Barzuq must give in. He *has* to give in. All we have to do is hold out, keep our nerve and keep the boy alive. We've done it now, there's no going back: that fat dog is our trump card. His worthless life is going to buy the lives of the comrades, and if Allah wills, we'll stretch it a bit further and buy ours as well. But their lives come first and therefore his does too. We will kill him only if Barzuq goes ahead with the executions. *Wallahi.*"

Chapter 4

THAT NIGHT AMBASSADOR and Mme. Levesque were giving
dinner at the Québécois Residence in al-Mazar. With their
son's schoolfriend still in the hands of guerrillas and with the
whole of the foreign community in an uneasy state of
suppressed panic they neither of them felt much like having
a party. However, it had been arranged weeks beforehand in
honor of various old acquaintances who would be passing
through al-Mazar at the same time and it would have been
difficult to cancel at this late stage. Of course—as Mme.
Levesque told her guests when they arrived—they *could*
have put everybody off because they were all old family
friends who would have understood. But then she'd thought
about it and she and Philippe and Bernard had all agreed that
cancelling the dinner would not have helped Wayne in the
slightest. It did no good to sit around and mope, did it?

Her guests were a mixed crew. There was M. le Duc de
Chevelle, a bald and melancholy French aristocrat who
roamed the world continuously in search of something to do.
There were two of M. Levesque's diplomatic colleagues:
Walter Slesinger, the Québécois Ambassador to Bangladesh
and his wife Kay, who were on their way home after a four-
year stint in Dacca. There was a Quebec army man, Colonel
Pat Forsyth, who was military attaché in Zibala for as long as

it took him to sell the Zibalan Air Force some jet fighters. And there was Damian.

Damian was a spaced-out young man whom Bernard had once found himself sitting next to on an Air India flight to New Delhi. He had attracted Bernard's attention by claiming to see Christ walking on the port wing thirty-three thousand feet above Kashmir. Additionally, he had scorned the lavish luncheon which was served to all the other First Class passengers, calling instead for a large plate of plain brown rice. Damian turned out to be a sessions musician who played the electric organ on the records of pop groups who couldn't play their own. He knew dozens of pop stars intimately and had enthralled Bernard all the way to New Delhi with gross stories of their private lives.

Bernard came downstairs wearing a dark suit and an Yves Saint-Laurent tie.

"How good-looking he is," said Kay to Mme. Levesque. "My, he looks just like his father used to."

"You're too kind," said Mme. Levesque coldly.

"How *extremely* good-looking he is," said the bald Duke mournfully to himself.

"Hi, man!" said Damian to Bernard. "How you doin'?"

"Ah, Bernard, there you are," said his father. "Perhaps you wouldn't mind seeing how people's drinks are getting on?"

"My poor boy," said Kay Slesinger, giving Bernard her empty glass and enclosing his hands in her own. "What an awful time it is for you."

"It's worse for Wayne."

"Oh, I don't know," said Kay, emphasizing her words with little pumps of Bernard's hands, which made the flesh on her dimpled forearms quake. "I think it's just as bad for those who have to sit at home and wait. It's the *not knowing* which is so terrible. At least your poor friend is in the know."

"If he's still alive," said Bernard. Kay shook her head vigorously.

"Now you mustn't say such a thing," she cried. "You'll only

make it worse for yourself. Besides, what good is he to them if he's dead? Think positively, that's what Wally and I have learned after all these years. Some of the places he's been posted to . . . well, you know what I mean." She lowered her voice until it was an intense whisper. "Don't let them get you down," she said. "Don't give them that satisfaction. And that was just a wee Martini with a tiny twist of lemon," she added, increasing the pressure on Bernard's hands until he thought the glass he held would break.

But Mrs. Slesinger had unknowingly expressed a general feeling of awkwardness, Bernard decided as he went from guest to guest mixing drinks as he had been taught. ("I do like a young man who knows how to mix a really dry Martini," Kay was confiding to the Duke. "They're getting rarer and rarer.") The truth is, went on Bernard to himself, none of them knows how to treat me. They don't know whether to act as though I'm bereaved or merely anxious. Should they commiserate or be trying to reassure me?

The only person who seemed to strike a relaxed note was Damian. It was true that he had never met Wayne, but even so he seemed oddly unconcerned.

"What an experience, man," he said. "It must be great to be out there in the desert some place with those guerrillas. I envy your friend: he's putting in some real time." He allowed Bernard to get him another glass of mango juice. Then he asked: "What are the cops like here?"

Bernard shook his head. "Lazy. Brutal. Cops, you know?" He shrugged. "But Dad says they have a pretty good idea what goes on because they've got thousands of informers. He reckons it's one of the advantages of having a country as poor as this: there are plenty of people who'll give information to the police for a few cents. Dad reckons they've probably got the guerrillas' families already and anybody else who knows them at all, and that it's just a matter of time before they catch the guerrillas themselves. If you leave aside the desert, there aren't that many places in

Zibala where they could be. Dad's got a bet on with the First Secretary Political at the Embassy that it's the police who get to them first and not the army."

"Yeah." Damian seemed not to have been giving Bernard his full attention. "But what I mean is, man, what are they like here about you know, hash, junk, stuff like that? Fact is, I've got a bit of a hassle on about . . ." A Zibalan in a white coat chose that moment to announce dinner, so Bernard excused himself to take Mrs. Slesinger by one plump arm to escort her into the dining room. "Little prick," murmured Damian into his mango juice.

But he perked up when he found that Mme. Levesque, the perfect hostess, had remembered his vegetarian eating habits. Conversation seemed to languish again with the change of room, so Damian gave a lengthy account of working with a group called Filthy Lucre in England. It appeared that he had been standing in for a member of the band who was sick. Unfortunately, the group's leader, Mick Macree, had been arrested in mid-act during an open-air rock concert at a stately home in the summer. The concert had come to a premature end; the fans had rioted, and one of Damian's fingers had been fractured when the stage was stormed by a mass of fighting policemen and youths. This had plunged Damian and his legal advisers into a prolonged wrangle over whether to sue Mick Macree, the British police, the lord whose stately home it was, Filthy Lucre or the man who had organized the concert.

"But why was Mr. Macree arrested?" Kay Slesinger wanted to know. Damian became evasive.

"Oh, just his stage routine," he said. "But they were filming it for television and you know how uptight the media are."

"I expect he took his clothes off?" said Kay hopefully.

"Quite early on," Damian assured her. "It was what he did later that made the cops interfere."

"*Ils sont des sauvages, ces jeunes,*" said the Duke from the other end of the table. "They should horsewhip them."

"That reminds me," began Colonel Forsyth firmly. "Did I ever tell you about when we were trying to help the Central Africans get something like a decent army together? They were an eager enough bunch, but they couldn't get used to the idea of modern warfare. They were accustomed to the old bush hand-to-hand stuff; you know, look your man in the eyeball and bop him one on the head with your cudgel. So we sold 'em a couple of squadrons of tanks and you should have seen their faces light up." The Colonel beamed around at his listeners. "Couldn't wait to go. They spent six months crashing around Central Africa in them—wrote off a few, I must say—until they'd pretty much got the hang of it. In fact by the time I left there were some damned good tank crews in Central Africa.

"But do you know a funny thing? Try as we might, we just couldn't break their old habit of taking whips along with them. They'd got so used to riding around on horseback or zebra-back or something they would feel naked without their whips. You'd see them roaring along at thirty miles an hour with this black fellow sticking up out of the hatch, lashing the armor-plating for all he was worth with a damn great leather thong. It was a pretty funny sight," the Colonel ended lamely.

Bernard glanced discreetly at his watch under cover of the edge of the table and raised an eyebrow at his father. M. Levesque nodded imperceptibly and whispered something to the splendidly-robed servant who had been standing like a statue just inside the door. The man bowed and went out, to return presently bearing a radio on a circular brass tray.

"Would you all think it very rude . . . ?" asked the Ambassador, leaving the question unfinished.

"Of course not," cried Kay Slesinger who, Bernard had noticed, was keeping the wine servant uncommonly busy. "Poor dear Bernard must know about his friend. Do turn it on, Philippe, it must be news time."

The kidnapping was still the lead item of the BBC World Service.

"There is still no news of Wayne Bulkeley, the MOPEC executive's son who was kidnapped yesterday by a group of Arab guerrillas in Zibala. Despite extensive mobilization of the Zibalan armed forces, no clues to the boy's whereabouts have yet been found, although our correspondent in the capital, al-Mazar, reports that it is widely believed he is still somewhere inside the country. It is now twenty-four hours since the self-styled Seventh January group, who are connected with the PLO, claimed responsibility for taking the boy. They say they are holding him pending the release from prison in Zibala of five of their members who are awaiting execution for acts of sabotage. The President of MOPEC, Mr. Harry Papasian, has described the kidnapping as 'an abhorrent and cowardly act by yet another bunch of International Marxist hooligans.' He has offered the sum of one hundred thousand dollars for the boy's release."

Suddenly the announcer—who had no doubt read the same bulletin several times already in the last few hours—changed his tone. The pitch of his voice went up slightly as he continued:

"We have just learned that the kidnappers have broken their silence. In the last hour Radio Zibala has been reported as saying the guerrillas are demanding the release of the five prisoners by midday tomorrow, local time. The guerrillas have threatened to cut off one of the boy's toes if their deadline is not met and to continue cutting off one toe for each hour's delay after the deadline has expired. They also threaten that if any of their comrades is harmed Wayne Bulkeley will be immediately shot.

"This news comes to you in the World Service of the BBC."

Bernard's father abruptly switched the radio off and put it on the floor beside him. Everyone's eyes, which had been on the perforated disc of its loudspeaker, turned involuntarily to Bernard's face and then away again. The old Duc de Chevelle broke the silence.

"Animals," he said. *"Ceux ne sont que des sauvages."*

"Don't worry, dear," said Kay Slesinger to Bernard, "they won't do anything to him."

"How the hell do you know?" asked Bernard rudely. He looked pale, and his right hand, which was holding a fragment of bread, was trembling slightly. Adult eye met adult eye across the table.

"Because," said his father gently, "the President will back down."

"How can you be so sure?" cried Bernard. "You're always telling us that dealing with Ismail Barzuq is like dealing with a child of ten, he's so unpredictable."

"Mais oui," agreed his father in a reasonable voice, "that's perfectly true. But when I say that, I'm only referring to what it's like for me to deal with him on a diplomatic level. I don't deny he's often exasperating the way he changes his mind; but in a thing like this he's quite capable of being a statesman. He can't afford to fool about. He knows very well that his own position as President is at stake if he messes this up. No, he'll give in."

"Of course he will," agreed Colonel Forsyth. "And if he looks like giving any nonsense I'll just go and tell him that Quebec has changed *its* mind about selling him the airplanes he wants. That'll fix him."

"Cutting toes off by the hour," Damian was musing down the other end of the table. His eyes were shining. "Man, that's rare."

"Well," said Bernard's mother brightly, "thank goodness for *some* news at any rate. When is the deadline? Midday tomorrow, wasn't it? I feel certain that poor Wayne will be back well before those fifteen hours are up. I just feel it, somehow."

"So do I, Renée," agreed Kay Slesinger. "I think feelings like that can so often turn out to be right, don't you?"

Bernard groaned inwardly. A flurry of servants brought in the main course: roast quails from the desert, stuffed with a mixture of garlic, dates and olives.

"Darling, Renée, you do spoil us. I feel like a queen."

"I agree," said M. le Duc, his melancholia seeming to have lightened somewhat.

"Oh," began Damian as he was served. "Uh, I'm a veg . . . oh"—his tone changed to one of amazement "oh." The "quail" on his own plate was revealed to be made of rice held together by a single leaf of Zibalan cabbage and modelled into a perfect replica of a roast bird. It had even been stuffed.

"Oh *bravo*, Renée," exclaimed Kay. "Don't I always tell you, Wally? Renée's the best hostess I know. Wherever she is, she always gets the best cook in town."

"Most ingenious," said the Colonel approvingly. "Damned clever thing for a Zib . . . for a, um, dinner party. I wonder if the fellow's had any military training? He'd be wonderful at camouflage. Or in his case you might call it *cabbage*-flage." He looked expectantly around with his eyebrows raised in a pained way.

To Bernard the meal dragged on in a seemingly endless series of courses, although there were only the usual five. His father chatted to de Chevelle about tax avoidance in France. Colonel Forsyth and Walter Slesinger could be heard reminiscing about arms sales they had clinched around the world. Kay Slesinger wanted to know how Renée Levesque managed to get such brilliant cooks while Damian launched into yet another of his showbiz tales.

"Dave was completely stoned," he kept saying. Bernard nodded politely. As soon as the meal was over and everyone had left the table for coffee, Damian drew Bernard aside.

"I guess I could fix it," he said craftily. "That is, if you're interested."

"Fix what?" asked Bernard blankly. Damian shook his head.

"Don't you listen, man? About what I was telling you. Dave needs someone with contacts to ease things on his tour next summer. You know, someone who can arrange beds for the group and square the hotel management for breakages when they leave, generally keep them out of the hair of the law. Their road manager doesn't know anyone on the ground in Quebec, and he can't speak French. With your father's contacts and your French, you'd be perfect. And the pay would be really something, you know. Nobody goes hungry working for Dave. Interested?"

"Well," Bernard began. "I suppose it sounds possible."

"You'd get into all their concerts, of course," said Damian. "Veep treatment. You'd go on the road with them wherever they went in Quebec, travel on Dave's Lear jet. If you played your cards right, it could be the start of something for you; Dave's got a few contacts of his own, you'd better believe. How about it?"

"Could you really fix it?" Bernard asked with a glimmer of interest. Damian tilted his head to one side.

"I don't see any problem. Provided I've got out of Zibala by then, of course," he added. "I may be languishing in jail here."

Bernard laughed. "You in jail here? Not a chance. Golly, nobody goes to jail in Zibala if they can afford the price of a bribe. Only the poor go to jail. Why should you be inside, in any case?"

"Like I was telling you earlier," said Damian earnestly. "There's this hash I've got. Man, have you tried this Zibalan stuff? It's wicked, the best ever. I want to take some home with me. Tell me straight, you've got the contacts: What are the chances of fixing the guys at the airport? It shouldn't cost too much, should it? Bit of diplomatic leverage, you know? Fix me my hash and I'll fix you your summer on tour with Dave. How about that?"

As soon as he could, Bernard made his excuses and went upstairs. He knew his departure had been abrupt but he did

not care: there was a limit to how much he could stand. He
shut his bedroom door and sat down on the edge of his bed.
Nobody actually gave a damn—that was what it came down
to. Was it going to go on like this forever? Heavy meals,
heavy wheels and heavy deals. He thrust his hands into his
jacket pockets and hunched forward miserably. Then he got
up and went over to the window, gazing sadly out.

In the well-lit street outside the Residence he could see an
unusually strong detachment of police guards standing
about. The whole of the immediate neighborhood which
housed the diplomatic community of al-Mazar was no doubt
similarly patrolled. It was nearly the only area in the city
which was properly lit, whose pavements did not have huge
gaps and missing manhole covers and whose inhabitants did
not trip over families asleep on the curbside when they came
home late at night. The police were indeed zealous about
keeping it free of beggars since it left them the sole
beneficiaries of a community generous with its small change.
God knew they needed any extra they could get, thought
Bernard, on a salary equivalent to thirty dollars a month.

He sighed. His right hand encountered a piece of paper in
his pocket which he brought out and glanced at absentmindedly. It was something Wayne had passed him in school
one day, a sketch of their history teacher in full swing. It was
a brilliant caricature. Bernard was conscious of a pang of
envy. Wayne had got the man exactly, just as he had so many
other people at school. Somehow he always managed to
bring out a ludicrous quality in any person he drew, deflating
the pretentious and mocking the serious. Bernard had never
quite managed to work out why he admired Wayne, but it
was perhaps for this artistic talent which made him—in his
eyes—dangerously anarchic. Nobody was ever quite safe
from Wayne, and it gave him an impulsive, unruly quality
which was notably absent in the generally cautious
diplomatic world. Besides, thought Bernard, it must be

marvelous to be able to draw like that and make people laugh.

Suddenly his mind went back to when he had last seen his friend. This was the first time since the kidnapping that he had been able to think about what had happened in the tower. Now, inexorably, every word of their argument came back to him. With brutal clarity he could hear himself calling Wayne by his nickname. Bernard went back and lay down on his bed. Then, the ferocity and suddenness of the attack taking him utterly by surprise, he turned onto his stomach and began to cry uncontrollably.

Later that night Ismail Barzuq met his Prime Minister's Cabinet in session. The Cabinet office, which was in the parliament building the British had built as a leaving present for Zibala on its independence, was modelled on the British Prime Minister's in London. The Zibalan version had imitation Louis Quinze chairs whose satin upholstery was covered in transparent plastic. The enormous table of Burmese teak was littered with coffee cups and tea glasses with cheap aluminum spoons embedded in the inch or so of undissolved sugar at the bottom of each.

The eight men sitting around the table were sharing a rare moment of silence since the Minister for Internal Security had dropped his bombshell, which was that one of the five prisoners the Seventh January wanted released had been killed that afternoon by a prison guard.

"Who-gave-the-order?" asked the President for the second time, emphasizing each word with a stubby finger on the table top. "*I* gave no such order. Nobody said he was to be killed. Prime Minister, did you order him killed?"

"No, Mr. President," said the Prime Minister vehemently. "That is, I gave no direct order. Nobody did." He looked helplessly around the table at his colleagues. "But the man had been sentenced to death." He spread hairy hands in an eloquent gesture. "He was due to die. Perhaps he was trying to escape and fell downstairs? They sometimes do. Or an overzealous prison guard, perhaps? Some of those men are very keen, you know." But the President was no longer listening.

"It puts us in a very awkward position," he said. "I've just had a call from the Americans. That fool Ambassador Deedle is trying to twist our arms. You know, the usual threats: cutting off aid, no more spare parts for our tanks, votes of censure in the UN. I gave him the usual reply: at the first sign of interference I pack my bags and fly to Moscow and bang goes the Americans' Middle East Policy. I'd like to see Deedle try to explain *that* to the President of the United States." He smiled grimly. This was a game he understood.

"I tell you what we're going to do, gentlemen," he went on decisively. "For the moment the death of this prisoner must be a complete secret—that is vital. But we'll fix a definite execution date for the others; um . . . let's say Saturday at dawn. That will give their revolutionary friends three whole days to get the message that we're not soft. Perhaps one of you would announce it to the press and radio? By then we may have found these ninety-eighth December bastards or whatever they call themselves, in which case I'll hang them myself in Independence Square. If not, we'll call their bluff. I'm not being told what to do by a lot of weak-kneed foreign liberals who are only in this country to see what they can get out of it." And President Ismail Barzuq thumped the Cabinet table with his fist, making the little spoons rattle in the coffee cups and tea glasses.

Chapter 5

When Wayne himself had heard the announcement of the ultimatum on Tewfiq's radio, his first thought was that it concerned somebody else. He simply could not believe that the newsreader's measured sentences about Wayne Bulkeley's toes being cut off referred to himself. Besides, none of the group had set foot outside the cave, much less delivered any ultimatum. Tewfiq had ordered complete radio silence to ensure the secrecy of their position and now carried the Morse key in one of his pockets.

On the announcement's being translated, the men in the cave had been jubilant. Suddenly, as if meeting again after a lengthy separation, they grinned and shook hands with each other.

"You see," cried Farid to Wayne, "tomorrow our friends are free or your toes come off." He laughed uproariously and made sawing gestures in the air with an imaginary knife. His companions collapsed with mirth. A kind of light-headedness seemed to have possessed them, and they kept turning around and giggling, pointing at Wayne's feet. Wayne wanted—and indeed tried—to be sick but produced only a tablespoonful of warm bile. Tewfiq came over and squatted down in the dust beside him.

"Incredible," he said, "you're worth a hundred thousand dollars to someone." He shook his head and whistled. "Valuable puppy. Do you know this Mr. Papasian?"

"Of course not," said Wayne. "He's the President of MOPEC."

Tewfiq whistled again. "It's another world, isn't it?" he said to his men. "A complete stranger offers one hundred thousand dollars for the life of an unknown boy. Here, three hundred Zibalan peasants could live like kings for an entire year on that."

"That's not my fault," said Wayne. Tewfiq spat.

"If I thought it was," he said, "I'd cut more than your toes off."

Wayne had never been more miserable in his life. Apart from fear of what the morrow would bring, the desert night had lowered the temperature in the cave to a point where he was shivering continuously in his shirtsleeves, thin trousers and nylon socks. He was so hungry he felt sick. He was covered in filth and beginning to stink, which he found more demoralizing than almost anything else. Needless to say, nobody in the group had thought to bring essentials like toilet paper; everything had to be done with handfuls of sand including, Wayne noticed with contempt, an imitation of "washing" which had no more than ritual significance. He knew that devout Moslems in desert regions often relied on sand instead of water for cleansing themselves at prayer times. Not that he had noticed any of his captors praying: nothing so active and deliberate. When not gleefully anticipating his mutilation, they merely sat or lay for hours at a stretch like animals chewing their cuds, neither asleep nor fully conscious but content simply to exist.

Yet Tewfiq had a lot to be worried about, Wayne decided as he lay in the dark of the cave. They had none of them eaten for nearly thirty-six hours. Tewfiq had ordered the water rationed to two liters each per day, an amount which sounded generous but which, given the heat in the cave from midday until early evening, was not. The living conditions were uniformly bad for everybody. Even the use of flashlights at night in the main cavern was banned. The men had grumbled, but Wayne could see from Tewfiq's point of view that he was right: any light in the cave would show for miles in an otherwise dark cliff face. Thus deprived even of a card game, the men had to rely on querulous chatting, dozing, or listening to endless Arab music on the radio. Even their tea had to be brewed in the depths of the passageway behind the cave.

Above all it was the hunger which nagged Wayne. Perhaps in a moment of objective honesty he would have agreed that, worse than the hunger itself, was the fear of being without food. He had grown up with his days structured by the necessity of much eating. There was breakfast, there were snacks, there was lunch, there was tea, there was dinner and there was usually a little something to take up to bed or— when he was in the U.S.—to nibble at while watching the late show on TV. The time of each meal was fixed and observed as strictly as if it had been a matter of religion. His mother's voice calling Wayne to the dining room was as much a summons as the muezzin's from the mosque. Thus had Wayne become a devout eater.

Now he lay awake and planned his escape. He dared delay no longer. If tomorrow he was likely to be mutilated piecemeal for something he had not done and did not fully understand anyway, he might as well take the chance. Tonight they had left him to sleep in a corner of the main cave while a couple of the men dozed by its entrance like watchdogs. Wayne had no idea of the time since Farid had long ago relieved him of his watch, an act which had caused some ill feeling among his comrades who clearly felt that the desert boots had been spoils enough and that someone else should get the watch.

He came up cautiously on one elbow. It was another moonless night, but a grey wash of starlight through the slit of the cave mouth enabled him to see the dark huddles of the sleeping men. He had no illusions about getting past Ibrahim and Farid: he knew he would never make it. He was pinning his hopes on an alternative, one which he had only noticed late that afternoon.

In the corner of the cave nearest to him, a niche had been carved into the soft sandstone wall. It might have been made a thousand years ago when the caves were occupied by desert people in hiding from marauders; probably it had been cut out to enable a couple of people to sleep slightly apart from their sheep and goats who were doubtless penned into the main cave with them. However, at some stage there had been an attempt to destroy the flat area thus carved out; either that or it had crumbled of its own accord. There was now not enough left of it to sleep one person comfortably. But Wayne, lying on his back in the long hours of the afternoon, had seen that there was a sizeable hole in the roof of the niche, much like a chimney above an old-fashioned hearth. It was invisible to anyone standing up, which was no doubt why none of his captors had noticed it. To Wayne it looked less like a flaw in the rock than a deliberately constructed hole: hopefully an emergency exit made by the cave's erstwhile inhabitants who had not wished to hide in a place from which they could not escape. He now proposed to put this theory to the test.

To say that he was frightened was not an adequate description. He was just short of being paralyzed completely by fear. It seemed to him that everything was happening in the kind of nightmare where some hideous risk has to be taken but where the horror of actually escaping seems worse than that of being caught in the act. As he drew himself slowly into a half crouch on the cave floor, Wayne found himself almost wishing that a flashlight would snap on and all hell break loose. At least it would absolve him from having to make any more nervous effort.

But no flashlight came on, and he began crawling across the sand towards the niche, prepared at any moment to roll over and groan as if disturbed in sleep or being ill. When he reached the niche and still nothing had happened, Wayne knew that the moment had come. As soon as he stood up and tried to climb into the hole, he would unequivocally be escaping: no amount of pretense would help. He waited another minute to postpone the inevitable, but instead of allowing his nerves to calm, it merely increased the tension. Moving with infinite care he climbed up onto the remains of the sandstone bench.

Standing, he found that the upper part of his body was entirely inside the chimney. Feeling around, he discovered a ledge at chin height, a flat area which extended at least beyond the reach of his outstretched arm. He glanced down and, now that his eyes were becoming accustomed to the almost pitch-darkness in the hole, was alarmed to see his trouser legs and stockinged feet gleaming palely in the starlight. It was now or never. Gingerly he drew one foot up, found a protruding knob of rock, and levered himself upwards into the hole.

Physical agility was not one of Wayne's attributes. He had always disliked bodily effort and was reduced in school to a flabby inertia, goaded by the teacher and mocked by his classmates. With a kind of bravado he had protected himself by cultivating a clumsiness so extreme it was comic, enraging his instructors by hanging like a sack of corn from ropes and wall bars, unable to raise himself a centimeter, and blundering full tilt into vaulting-horses instead of springing over them like everybody else. Now as he tried to heave himself upwards in silence, he wished that he had developed a rudimentary muscle or two. His arms, not strong at the best of times, were watery from the additional weakness of not having eaten. Eventually, though, he found himself flat on his face, trying to stifle his heavy breathing, while he pulled a remaining leg up behind him. Then he stood up, listening.

He had made surprisingly little noise. No loose stones or falls of dust had come thumping down into the cave below. From up in the chimney he could hear no sounds from the sleeping men. He felt around in the darkness for his next direction. He found it in the same place as the first: another seemingly giant step upwards cut into the rock. Wearily he pulled himself up once again.

As he lay gasping on his stomach for the second time, he suddenly felt something scrabble under his hand. Visions of snakes and scorpions filled his mind, and involuntarily he gave a little cry of fear and disgust, jerking his hand back. As he did so, he dislodged a stone. Horrified, he heard it strike a nearby wall and then bounce down onto the ledge he had just left. With his heartbeat making a loud noise at the back of his throat, Wayne lay not knowing whether he was more afraid of the viciously poisonous creatures which no doubt lurked ahead or of the men below, who even then must be waking up and reaching for their automatic weapons.

But miraculously there were still no sounds of disturbance. The stone he had knocked obligingly failed to drop down into the cave itself, so Wayne climbed to his feet and struck his head stunningly against the low rock ceiling. A blaze of light filled his skull, and he dropped back into a crouch, clenched around the pain and rocking in silent agony while tears squeezed between his eyelids. When he could bring himself to relax and wipe his eyes on his shirtsleeve, he edged cautiously foward, one hand outstretched in front of him. Gingerly he rounded a bend in the cramped tunnel in which he found himself, and there, at a slight downward angle, was something which at last gave him hope: a distinct patch of grey light.

Bent double and still with one hand thrust out, Wayne moved down the slight slope towards it. It turned out to be framed by a narrow opening in the rock, a hole which gave access to a sandy floor about five feet beneath, as far as he could judge. Getting a grip on the surrounding rock, he attempted to lower himself down at arm's length, but here his muscles failed him. Slithering rapidly through the hole, Wayne fell heavily to the floor beneath.

As he fell, he thought he heard a distant shout, but sitting on the cold sand and checking himself for broken bones, he put it down to his own voice gasping in surprise. He got to his feet and found himself in a small cave lit, like the larger one he had left, by starlight. This time, however, the cave mouth was almost circular and, Wayne saw, was accessible from the outside by a tiny path little better than a ledge. The guerrillas' cave presumably lay to the right of this one and slightly higher up the cliff face.

Now that he had a real chance of getting away, Wayne realized that he had only one choice. He must reach the oasis and contact the local police or the headman. Looking out across the starlit plain, Wayne could see Bir Huzun quite clearly as a dark stain: there were even one or two welcoming yellow gleams of oil lamps barely visible. From the base of the cliff the oasis was perhaps no more than three-quarters of a mile away, but at present it lay three or four hundred feet beneath where he stood. He leaned out and looked at the track down which he knew he would have to go. In daylight it would have seemed a moderately insane climb to attempt even though the track must have been regularly used by whoever had once lived in the caves. At nighttime, however, it was utterly mad to try it, except that there was the single advantage that the worst drops and gulfs remained invisible. Yet the mere act of having escaped his prison had improved Wayne's morale considerably, and with the knowledge that at least he had a good head for heights, he edged himself around the corner of the cave mouth and began picking his way down the cliff face.

As he did so, he thought once again that he heard a distant shout. He froze for another ten seconds, pressing himself against the rock; but when he heard no further sound, he put it down to imagination and concentrated on getting down to the ground in one piece.

It turned out to be a long, nerve-racking, but not very difficult climb. There was one heart-stopping moment when the remains of one of his nylon socks snagged on a spur of rock and he had tottered, arms flailing, on the brink of a crevasse. Limp with reaction, he gingerly reached down and shucked off what was left of both socks, letting them float down instead to the tumbled boulders below. His feet were, he knew, cut and torn in several places, but in the cold they were largely numb and the additional margin of safety being barefoot gave him was worth the loss of what had been at best the flimsiest protection.

Finally, and almost with disbelief, Wayne reached the bottom. He came down the final slope feeling exhilarated and almost athletic; he even jumped the last couple of feet onto the desert floor and then walked backwards away from the cliff, looking up at what he had just descended.

"Well," he said out loud to himself, "there are some people who simply would not believe you climbed down that. I don't think old Bernard would have done it himself at any price." He suppressed a giggle, for he was becoming almost lightheaded with elation. "Old Bernard," Wayne told the desert, "would have got his father to send in a UN task force to winch him down. Either that or he'd have made a formal request for the Zibalan army to dismantle the cliff until he could be flown off by Quebec Air Force helicopters." Wayne was rather enjoying himself. Giving a last giggle, he turned and set off for the oasis whose nearest edge now seemed hardly any distance away. He was just passing the last spur of rock before the level desert began when a familiar voice spoke from its shadow.

"Off to market, Fatty?" asked Tewfiq.

Wayne gave a little squeal of terror and began to run, heavily, hopelessly, his feet slowed by the paralyzing nightmare which had at last caught up with him. He felt a hand reach for his collar, and then Tewfiq threw him easily to the desert floor and kicked him in the stomach.

"Poor Fatty," he said. "Did you think you'd got away?" He lugged Wayne by his hair into a sitting position. The boy lolled in his grasp, his hands pressed to his stomach, his mouth a soundless O, savagely winded. His breath came back just before he thought he would die of asphyxiation, and with it the renewed fear and hopelessness that for one blissful moment he believed he had escaped.

Tewfiq sat beside him on the ground until Wayne's paroxysm of crying was over. Then he said conversationally:

"You know you really disgust me the way you cry?"

"And do *you* know," said Wayne, snuffling mucus on to his shirtsleeve, "I don't give a damn?"

To his surprise he heard Tewfiq laugh shortly, then felt himself hauled to his feet.

"Back we go," said his captor. "I must say," he remarked as he prodded Wayne back up the path down which he had so recently come, "that was really quite a climb. I am impressed. That took good nerves. Were you afraid?"

Wayne, still slightly bent with the pain in his stomach, found enough pride to say, "No, not particularly."

"Good," said Tewfiq.

"What do you mean, 'good'?" demanded Wayne. "I didn't climb all that way to earn a commendation from you for moral bravery: I was trying to avoid having my toes cut off by moral cowards." Again he was surprised that no blow followed. "When did you discover I had gone?" he wheezed.

"I didn't, Farid did. He was woken by some noise you must have made, but it took us time to find out how you'd gone. You did well to find that hole; none of us knew it was there. Congratulations," said Tewfiq. "It will not happen again."

"I bet," said Wayne leadenly.

"And once we knew how you'd gone, it wasn't difficult to work out where you'd be going to," said Tewfiq as though he had not heard. "Obviously, there was only one place you could go to: Bir Huzun. Unfortunately you were not to know that it wouldn't have helped you."

"I don't see why not," said Wayne.

"You don't see anything," Tewfiq told him with a sudden

return of his former mood. "You're just a stupid damned foreigner."

"I can't know any better unless somebody tells me," said Wayne hotly. "At least if you're going to kill me and . . . and cut bits off me you might just tell me what the hell is going on, and who you really are, and what you hope to achieve, and why me anyway." Instinctively he cringed, waiting for the blow which would surely follow this outburst, but still none came. On the other hand, neither did an answer. Tewfiq kept propelling him silently upwards. About halfway up the cliff they made a course change onto a path which Wayne had not known existed and which cut up a steep defile almost directly to the clear area where they had first arrived in the Land Rover. Presently they were back in the cave.

"It's okay," said Tewfiq in Arabic as they felt their way in. "I've got him. No flashlights," he added hurriedly.

"Little bastard," said Farid, leaping forward out of the darkness and cuffing Wayne a stinging blow on the side of the head. Wayne staggered back and then felt Tewfiq thrust his way between them.

"Enough," he ordered. "We've got him back. There's no harm done."

"At least tie the son of a whore up," suggested Adil. "*Ya ibn sharmuta*," he said to Wayne to make the matter quite clear.

They found some cord in the bag in which the Primus stove had come and tied Wayne's elbows behind him. Then they tied his ankles and ran the cord loosely back up to his elbows. None of the knots was tight enough to interfere with his circulation, Wayne discovered, but the trick of tying his elbows rather than his wrists meant that there was no way in which he could reach the knot. Thus hobbled he was pushed to the opposite corner of the cave from the one he had previously occupied. Exhausted with the effort and reaction, Wayne fell asleep almost at once, seeing his captors settling down again into watchful poses in the grey predawn light.

At a few minutes after nine he was awoken by a violent blow. He looked up to see Farid gazing down at him.

"Today we do some cutting, *mush kida?*" the man announced pleasantly. "The news is not good for you."

Wayne saw that the rest of the group were sitting, unshaven and serious-faced, around Tewfiq's radio.

"Barzuq is playing a dangerous game," said Tewfiq when the bulletin was over. His colleagues had turned hostile faces to watch Wayne as he struggled against the cord. "The President says that he will execute our comrades this Saturday at dawn."

"Unless what?" asked Wayne from his corner.

Tewfiq spat. "Unless nothing," he said. "Just that."

"You mean he doesn't intend to release them?"

"What do you think?" said Tewfiq. "It sounds as if you're going to start losing toes as from midday today."

"For heaven's sake," said Wayne in a panic, "you surely can't mean to go through with that? What's the good, anyhow? Barzuq can't possibly know whether you're actually cutting my toes off or not. I know it was just a bluff on your part—it was just a stage in the bargaining to try and convince Barzuq you weren't fooling."

Tewfiq looked at him in a way which made Wayne shrivel up inside. "You're so wrong," he said at length. He nodded downwards in the direction of Bir Huzun. "I shall cut your toe off at midday and it will be on Barzuq's desk by six o'clock this evening; make no mistake. We're not amateurs, you know; this is something involving many people which we have been planning for months. How do you imagine we delivered our ultimatum?"

"I suppose you must have radioed someone," said Wayne.

"Wrong," Tewfiq told him. "The only call we have sent out was a coded message of four groups before it was even officially known you were missing. You saw me send it less than half an hour after we had got you. I had to tell Daoud Hafez that we had snatched someone, but that it was you and not Levesque."

"How did you know my name?" asked Wayne sullenly.

"We'd been watching Levesque for weeks. We knew the names of all his friends and contacts. We knew his habits. We knew, for instance, that you usually went riding together at Assuf on Mondays. It was just a question of knowing someone in the stables who could tell us that you had gone to Ramla rather than Wadi Ain, say."

"Very clever," said Wayne. "So very clever that after all that you got me instead of Bernard. So much for your brilliant intelligence work."

Tewfiq eyed him speculatively, perhaps wondering whether to get up and hit him.

"I admit," he said at length, "we slipped up. The men actually doing the job"—he motioned to Sami and Farid—"were not familiar enough with how you and Levesque looked. That was a bad mistake. You're certainly easy to tell apart," he added, with unintentional cruelty.

"All right, then, how did you deliver the ultimatum?" Wayne asked, his curiosity aroused.

"Daoud Hafez did that. It was all arranged beforehand. He is not even inside Zibala. Once he knew we'd got you, he had someone call Radio Zibala anonymously. They checked with the U.S. Embassy, confirmed you'd been kidnapped, and made the announcement. That was easy. We have found it is the safest way to negotiate: we let people outside the country do it for us. That way we don't get caught leaving messages or having our telephone lines tapped. Once the operation's in motion, the whole thing is out of our hands."

"You sound like a big organization," said Wayne. It occurred to him that if he had to be captured at all he would rather it was by some highly organized and notorious gang than by a disaffected group of Zibalan peasants.

"We are," said Tewfiq with pride. "Seventh January is a fighting force people will have to take notice of where any Middle Eastern politics are concerned."

"But surely having someone else run your operations from outside the country means that if anything goes wrong at your end you are out of touch with this leader of yours, whoever he is?"

Tewfiq shook his head. "No," he said. "Daoud Hafez can always reach me on this"—he indicated the radio—"either on shortwave or by means of prearranged phrases worked into an ordinary broadcast. In a real emergency I can break radio silence and get a message to him. But we all know that on an operation we use our own initiative. That's what being a freedom fighter means."

"Oh," said Wayne.

They all lapsed into a silence which lasted nearly two hours and which Wayne broke twice, once to ask if Tewfiq could untie him and the second time to inquire fretfully about food. Behind the pain of his bruised stomach and the fear of what was shortly to happen to him, there was an increasingly demanding emptiness.

"Don't you ever get hungry?" he finally asked the men at large in Arabic. "Don't any of you feel it would be nice to get your teeth into some warm freshly baked bread? Or are you all too stupid to know when you're hungry?"

Wayne hadn't meant it to come out like that; it had just slipped out in the despair of the moment. Overcome with horror at his own foolishness he lay and waited for the retribution he knew must follow: the slaps, the kicks, the punches. Farid sprang to his feet with an oath and reached for the knife in his belt, but Tewfiq was equally quick. Almost without seeming to move from his position on the ground, he tripped Farid and had disarmed him before Farid knew what was happening. Enraged, the man struggled, but Tewfiq held him in what was obviously an agonizing hold, making the noises hostlers make to restive horses. Gradually Farid stopped resisting and relaxed, and Tewfiq broke the hold. The others had watched impassively.

"That's what he wants," Tewfiq told Farid earnestly. "He's not as stupid as he looks. You see, lying trussed up like a plump fowl in the corner he has managed to get us fighting among ourselves."

"I want him, Tewfiq," said Farid. "For the sake of my honor you must let me have him."

"*Lissa badri*. We wait."

Wayne, relieved that he was not immediately to be torn limb from limb for his temerity, reflected on this episode in astonishment. Tewfiq was wrong—he had had no idea of causing dissent in the group. But now he had seen how easy it was, Wayne began to envisage possibilities. He had failed to escape, but maybe he could yet cause the men to fall out and stop functioning as an efficient unit. In any case there were already obvious disagreements between them about what action to take. He remembered the conversation in which Tewfiq had asserted his authority over the group's two hard liners, Farid and Adil, who had wanted to kill him straight away.

At five to eleven Tewfiq tuned in the radio carefully to await a shortwave broadcast. So much Wayne could see from where he lay. He assumed it was a prearranged moment for the group to receive any instructions from their leader. The message came through, as far as he could judge, as part of a normal broadcast. Indeed, it seemed to be a Jordanian program about animal husbandry aimed at agricultural students. It clearly meant something to his captors, however, since after a low and tense discussion they came out of their huddle around the radio looking puzzled and angry. Farid especially seemed full of a smouldering rage. Tewfiq came over to Wayne and stood looking down at him.

"It seems you are . . . what's the expression? . . . temporarily reprieved," he said shortly.

"How do you mean?" asked Wayne anxiously.

"We have instructions to ignore the deadline at midday."

"He's told you not to cut my toe off?"

"We have been asked not to cut it off *yet*," corrected Tewfiq sourly. Then he turned and went back to his men.

Clearly, the news had taken them all by surprise. They disappeared around the corner into the passageway where Wayne had spent the first night and a bitter argument ensued. He could hear Farid's voice above the others although he could hear none of the actual words owing to the distorting effect of the cave. But the angry tone was unmistakable. Wayne knew only too well that Farid was demanding that Tewfiq ignore instructions and start to get tough. They, after all, were the ones on the ground actually carrying out the operation; they were the ones who stood to get killed for the kidnapping. One could not make a donkey like Barzuq give in unless he was forced to by foreign pressure, and the only way to get foreign pressure quickly was by lopping pieces off their hostage and sending them to the U.S. Ambassador in al-Mazar . . .

Thus Wayne unwillingly played devil's advocate against his own intense desire to pretend that nothing like this was being said. But he knew it was. He lay in his bonds and awaited the outcome.

Chapter 6

IN HIS EXECUTIVE suite atop the MOPEC headquarters, a sizeable piece of real estate in Manhattan, Harry Papasian took a call from his secretary.

"Sir," she said, "I have a Mr. Dwight Holmes from State on the line for you. Would you use the secure line, please?"

State Department were so damned security conscious they probably put their own laundry lists into cipher, thought Papasian crossly as he reached over and picked up the blue telephone. Harry Papasian had come from very little in Armenia and was now rather a lot in America: he thought of himself quite unashamedly and correctly as a good businessman. He had a considerable contempt for politicians, but the more successful he had become and the more of the world's oil market his company controlled, the more he was forced to play politics. It irked him badly.

"Yes, Dwight," he said into the phone.

"Look, Harry," his caller said without preamble. "Did you make that offer of one hundred grand to Daoud Hafez on your own account?"

"I did," said Papasian. "Although I'm damned if I see why I have to tell you that. It's my own company, my own money and my own business."

"Sure, Mr. Papasian," agreed Holmes in a conciliatory

voice. "Only we're getting a little concerned at this end about the way this kidnapping business is going."

"Well, I sure appreciate that concern," said Harry. With one hand he reached across his desk, fumbled the cap off a bottle and poured himself a glass of fizzy French mineral water, his sixth that morning. "We're a little bothered this end, too. Bulkeley's a MOPEC employee."

"Exactly. Who is he?"

"Oh," said Harry Papasian, sipping the water and savoring the delicious prickle of carbon dioxide inside his upper lip, "nobody. I had his file sent up. Good solid third ranker. We like him, apparently."

"So you offered one hundred thousand dollars to Daoud Hafez for his son's release? You realize that as far as we're concerned that's the thin end of the wedge? If you give him the money and he *maybe*—I stress *maybe*—releases the kid, the next thing we'll know is that every revolutionary Tom, Dick or Harry in the Middle East will kidnap some American employee's child, safe in the knowledge that he'll walk away with one hundred thousand bucks. State Department thinks this is a dangerous precedent to set. I take it you haven't yet paid the money?"

"Correct," said Harry Papasian tersely.

"Thank Heaven for that. Look, Harry, the general feeling here is that we'd be most obliged if you would withdraw your offer. The White House wants Barzuq to handle this affair himself. It's part of U.S. policy: the President's always boss in his own country. If that fails, we'll apply whatever pressure it takes; but if you don't mind my speaking honestly, it only louses up our hand if we have private individuals barging in and negotiating direct with the enemy. We don't talk to louts like Hafez."

Papasian heard him out in silence, his face impassive, now and again sipping the mineral water. Then he said:

"United States Government or not, nobody tells me who I can talk to, Holmes. I suggest the U.S. takes care of its own

affairs. Meanwhile, I'm running MOPEC. I'm not wet behind
the ears and I've got a lot of damned good advisers of my
own. I want Bulkeley's kid back: he's my employee and not
yours. I take it personally that this whole business was
directed against MOPEC, and I shall deal with it personally.
It's my responsibility. When I'm so decrepit and rubber-
toothed that I have to get State Department to negotiate on
my behalf I'll let you know. Meanwhile, Dwight—lay off."
And Harry Papasian hung up in triumph.

"That should hold him for a morning," he said to the
telephone. Then he buzzed his secretary. "Miriam, would
you get me Dan?"

When his personal aide came in, Harry Papasian said:

"Dan, I want a priority telex to Jim Cathcart in Amman. It
must be secure, understand? No international business codes
or anything dumb like that. Ready? Message reads:

CONTACT DAOUD HAFEZ SOONEST STOP RAISE OFFER TO
ONEFIFTY GRAND PAYABLE ANY CURRENCY ON IMMEDIATE
REPEAT IMMEDIATE RELEASE KID STOP EMPHASIZE POSITIVELY
LAST MOPEC OFFER OF ANY KIND EVER TO REBEL GUERRILLA
FREEDOM FIGHTER PRESIDENT KING PRINCE POPE DICTATOR OR
GOVERNMENT STOP TELL HIM HE CAN KIDNAP ME AND ENTIRE
BOARD OF DIRECTORS AND WILL STILL GET ZILCH . . .

You'd better amend that to

NOT ONE CENT ON STRICT INSTRUCTIONS CIRCULATED TO ALL
MOPEC EMPLOYEES WORLDWIDE STOP BANZAI STOP TOPDOG
MESSAGE ENDS

Got that?" Harry Papasian asked.

"Got it," said the aide. "I'll get that off right away, Mr.
Papasian."

"Fine. Don't ask me how I know, but I've got a feeling that
old bastard is hooked."

"Daoud Hafez?"

"Daoud Hafez. Money speaks Arabic, too. Any queries?"

"There is just one, Mr. Papasian. These 'strict instructions circulated to all MOPEC employees'—I don't seem to remember those."

"You don't," agreed Harry. "So circulate 'em."

By midmorning the heat in the cave was becoming intense. Wayne lay on the floor, the flies going in and out of the cave mouth—now suddenly iridescent as their wings caught the brilliant sunlight, now as suddenly invisible as they passed into the shadow of the overhang. The time dragged. The argument within the group had been settled somehow; the men now sat or lay sullenly waiting for instructions on the radio. Wayne could understand their mortification. By intervening, this leader of theirs, Daoud Hafez, had effectively taken command of the operation. The initiative had passed from the guerrillas' hands and now lay with Seventh January's leadership outside Zibala. Only Tewfiq seemed to be reasonably unperturbed by the change in tactics.

The old midday deadline came and went without anything more significant happening than Farid scowling at Wayne and fingering his knife blade and Tewfiq passing around the water ration. Something would have to happen soon, Wayne thought. They were now halfway through the water supply, and when that ran out in a couple of days' time, they would have to move or die. He wondered how his parents were. As far as they knew, he might even at this moment be bleeding like a stuck pig while his captors triumphantly held up one of his toes. At one o'clock the BBC noted that the deadline had passed, but could offer no confirmation about whether it had been met. The Seventh January were silent, it noted.

At two o'clock the BBC reported that Zibala's president, Ismail Barzuq, had unequivocally refused to release the five

condemned prisoners. "This is a free democracy," he was
quoted as having said at a press conference. "The people of
Zibala are not going to be blackmailed into running their
country to suit the whims of a group of Communist
terrorists. The rule of law will be upheld. The five prisoners,
who have been condemned to death after a fair trial, will be
shot at dawn on Saturday as previously announced. Nothing
can alter this irrevocable decision."

This provoked angry mutterings among the men. Tewfiq,
who for the first time was beginning to show signs of strain,
suddenly picked up his gun, cocked it and pointed it at
Farid's head.

"That's it!" he shouted. "I've had enough!" An immediate
silence fell as he glared at them over the unwavering muzzle.
"You've done nothing but mutter and grouse like a bunch of
old women. In case you've forgotten, we are at war. You are
soldiers, and I am your commanding officer until such time
as Daoud Hafez sees fit to relieve me of my post. You are not
fighting for yourselves, you are fighting for the Zibalan
people." He jerked a thumb over his shoulder towards the
mouth of the cave. "Right now we're fighting specifically for
the lives of five comrades in jail. Clear?"

The men shuffled their feet.

"I don't call this fighting," said Farid sullenly.

"Well, it is," retorted Tewfiq; "that's just where you're
wrong. Sitting here in this lousy cave is just as much fighting
as roaring around blowing up police stations. Do you know
why?" Farid was silent. "Because apart from anything else
just the five of us have tied up the larger part of the Zibalan
armed forces. Most of the police and army are going around
in circles out there trying to find us. It's not going to happen
yet—it's still too soon—but can't you see what that would
mean if the revolution was planned for tonight? The army
dispersed and preoccupied, the police trying to conduct
house-to-house searches, the Government thinking about

how best to save its face. We'd be home and dry before they knew what hit them."

"I suppose we have stirred them up a bit," admitted Ibrahim grudgingly.

"Stirred them up? They don't know whether they're coming or going. Behind those firm statements that dog Barzuq keeps putting out, there's complete confusion, believe me. He doesn't know what the hell to do; and the quieter we keep, the less he has to go on. What he really wants is for us to make a move and give him a lead. Well, we're not going to. We sit here and sweat. That is an order."

Tewfiq looked at his men and, holding the bolt of his weapon back with one hand, squeezed the trigger and slowly uncocked the gun. Then he leaned the weapon carefully against the cave wall and went back to sit by the opening, looking out towards where the oasis baked in the sun. Slowly the men dispersed and set about small tasks which kept their hands busy. Two of them got the Primus alight and a kettle on; the other two cleaned their guns.

Wayne had been lying all this time as if forgotten. Now, cramped and thirsty, he called weakly to Tewfiq.

"Untie me, please. I want to go to the bathroom."

Tewfiq gave an order and jerked his head at Sami who undid the knots and escorted Wayne to the passageway. Wayne was so weak and stiff that he had to lean against the wall. Then Sami led him back to the cave.

"If I'm to die of hunger, there are a few things I'd like to know first," he told Tewfiq. Tewfiq glanced up and looked him over.

"You won't die of hunger," he said. "I've never heard such a stupid idea. Look at that—" he reached up and to Wayne's shame gripped a fold of his stomach through his shirt. "There's a couple of months' living left on you. Don't talk to me about hunger. Do you feel any pain?"

"Only where you kicked me," said Wayne.

"Exactly. None of those agonies that novelists say will tie you into knots after a couple of days without food?"

"Well, no," admitted Wayne. Tewfiq smiled grimly.

"There won't be any," he said. "At one time or another each of my men has been without food for two, even three weeks. A week is nothing. Provided there is water, a healthy person needs very little food to keep going. Men fight better on empty stomachs, too. They are more alert."

"But it surely makes you too weak?" insisted Wayne.

"Not for the first fortnight. Tell the truth, how do you feel?"

It was such an unexpected question that for a moment Wayne was at a loss. He stood there, a mass of cuts and bruises and lumps, his face still caked with filth and dried blood, the side of his head tender and crusted, his throat feeling banded with dull purple weals.

"You feel," Tewfiq stated before he could reply, "rather well. I could say you haven't felt better in a long while. Sure, you've been roughed up a little, but that's just on the surface. Underneath, your body's beginning to get healthy. Don't deny it; it's true."

Confused and much wanting to turn the whole conversation away from this direction, Wayne mumbled assent. He could not deny that there was some truth in what Tewfiq said. His waistband already felt noticeably looser, and he remembered that brief moment of exhilaration after his night climb down the cliff path. He lay down beside Tewfiq and stared out at the desert.

"Who are you?" he asked at length. "What do you want?"

"Seventh January? It's simple; we want justice for the Zibalan people. We want more food, better houses, better pay, better working conditions, better schools and hospitals, all those. But above all we want an end to the corruption; it's that which hurts. We're not fools. *I* know Zibala can't afford the things we demand; the country's broke, everybody knows that. We're living on . . . on international charity, on big loans and handouts which the West gives us because it is too frightened of what might happen if Zibala collapses or goes Communist. But Seventh January believe we can live with a bad economy.

"Our organization was started by ordinary Zibalans but we now have support throughout the Arab world. We believe there has been more than enough talk about Marxism and socialism in the Middle East which has led to nothing. The PLO talks about Marxism and Egypt and Algeria and the rest talk about socialism; but the ordinary *fellah* on the land remains just as poor and just as ignorant and just as oppressed as ever. Seventh January says to hell with talk and let's get down to stopping some of the obvious injustice.

"What we in Zibala can't live with is our President behaving like a medieval king, our ministers and politicians like princes, our businessmen profiteering on the international aid to Zibala. We can't live with government contracts going to companies owned by the ministers themselves or their families. We can't see people living on the pavement while the rich live in air-conditioned villas. We can't see people driving around in imported Mercedes cars when in country places little children have to walk eight miles to school and eight miles back again—if there is a school, that is. We can't see peasants worked like animals on land owned by men who are always in New York, or Bonn, or London on business. We can no longer allow the police to swagger around like brutes, terrorizing the poor and fawning on the rich."

"Then it's true what Harry Papasian said about you?" broke in Wayne.

"What, that we're 'International Marxist hooligans'?"

"Yes. I mean, you must be Communists, or something."

Tewfiq shook his head. "Who knows?" he said. "To hell with labels. I went to the university in England and I've travelled in Europe and America and I've still never read more than about half a chapter of Marx, so I don't suppose

I'm a Marxist. We're not interested in all that intellectual stuff about the philosophy of economics; we're only interested in getting justice for the ordinary Zibalan. If it takes shooting the whole damned Government one by one, then that is what we'll do. We live only for the day when we can have a President who is enough a man of the people to live like one of the people. Just think if governments had to live like the people they governed: what an incentive *that* would be to improve the economy." Tewfiq fell silent.

"I know it's bad here," Wayne said timidly. Tewfiq merely snorted.

"You know nothing," he said. "Nothing. You foreigners are the same as our Government: you work for each other, not for Zibala. You live in a special area, eat your own imported food, drive your own cars and live your own lives as if you were really in America all along. What do you know of Zibala?"

"I've been to the *souk*; I've seen the people. I have eyes."

" 'I've been to the *souk*,' indeed. Every damned tourist goes to the *souk*. They go to buy things cheaper than they can get them at home and are congratulated by their friends for their cleverness. And what do they see? Wonderful picturesque people with their robes and bundles, engaging children with their big dark eyes and bare feet. Click! they go with their Polaroid cameras. Click! Click! Now they've done the *souks* of al-Mazar and they can go back to the Hilton or the Sheraton before they get their pockets picked or catch a disease. Pah!" Tewfiq spat disgustedly.

"It wasn't like that," Wayne protested. "I haven't even got a camera. I went to get away from home and learn a bit of Arabic. I've got friends in the *souk*. They keep a perfume shop."

"Yes, some of those shopkeepers do very well out of cultivating tourists."

Wayne looked at him in shocked surprise.

"You're a real cynic, aren't you?" he said. "As a matter of

fact I've never given them a cent except once to buy some jasmine essence for my mother. But I've visited them a dozen times since then and it's they who keep giving me things: tea and coffee and Zibacola. And as for them doing well, they live like animals. I've seen the way they live behind the shop and I wouldn't keep a dog like that. One tap between eight families, no bathroom, just an open sewer. Mud and cockroaches."

"Quite," said Tewfiq. "Time they had some hard cash off you, I should say. In any case, multiply that by several tens of millions, and that's my country." He waved a hand at the oasis again. "Have you . . ." but his words were suddenly drowned by a shattering roar. A huge helicopter appeared, framed in the cave opening, but travelling away from them or Tewfiq and Wayne would surely have been spotted. It had flown from behind them straight over the escarpment which had screened the sound of its approach. Now it hung in the air, rotor blades flashing, not more than fifty meters away. Instinctively, Tewfiq and Wayne had ducked down and crawled back on their stomachs. The machine was in the desert camouflage of the Zibalan Air Force and was close enough for the rows of rivets to be visible; Wayne could even see small pebbles caught between the treads of one of its tires. There was evidently a soldier sitting in the open doorway, for a pair of legs wearing combat fatigues and boots hung in space from one side.

Suddenly coming to his senses Wayne made a lunge forward, but he scarcely gained an inch against the restraining grip of Tewfiq's hand which, unnoticed, had fastened once more on the back of his shirt. Wayne sank back again, bitterly wondering how he could have been so stupid as to have made that fatal delay, to have forgotten that he badly wanted to be seen. Meanwhile the pilot, who was clearly not conducting a very serious or methodical search of the cliff face, moved slowly to another spot before abruptly swinging away and heading for the oasis. A little later they

watched the helicopter land close to the dense fringe of
palms, the wind from its rotors sending up ragged rolls of
dust. Two men in military uniform disembarked and
vanished among the trees, and then about a dozen troops
jumped down and strolled or lay in attitudes of relaxation
about the machine, their weapons loosely stacked against its
landing gear.

The rest of the group had long since joined Tewfiq and
Wayne on their stomachs at the cave mouth.

"What the hell's going on?" demanded Adil, who had been
woken by the noise.

"Anybody's guess," Tewfiq told him. "But you'll notice the
troops have been ordered to stay out of the village."

"So far," said Sami. "I wonder how long that'll last."

"They won't take on the Sheikh," said Ibrahim. "The
army's got enough problems of its own just now without
wanting to add to them."

"It depends on what sort of pressure Barzuq's under," said
Sami. "He may have told the army to act like an army."

"I agree with Ibrahim," said Tewfiq. "They're not here for
trouble. If they had been, they would have brought a lot
more men and some proper support. They don't know what
the villagers have got tucked away in that oasis."

Wayne could not make head or tail of all this, but it seemed
to him that he had asked enough questions for one day: the
mood of the men had become more tense since the arrival of
the helicopter. He lay with his head on his forearms, dozing,
while the sun dropped down the sky, turning orange and
appearing to expand as it neared the horizon. By the time
Tewfiq turned the radio on at halfpast six—presumably
another prearranged time—it was a huge distorted globe,
sagging slightly under its own weight as it rested on the rim
of the earth like an underinflated balloon. This time the
message came in an Arabic program about the conservation
of fishery stocks, and the men's attention and the shortness of

the time they listened made the gist of it explicit even to Wayne.

"Conservationists have long conceded," a woman was saying, "that fishermen often experience the greatest difficulty when fishing for one species which habitually consorts with another. Thus, an unwanted species may find itself snared in their nets. An example is the Pacific yellowfin tuna which often swims with schools of porpoises—which are air-breathing mammals. The porpoises become entangled in the tuna nets and drown. Under the Marine Mammal Protection Act of 1972 there is a yearly limit to the number of porpoises tuna fishermen can kill. Once that figure has been reached, the Act demands the immediate release of any live porpoises caught, with severe penalties for fishermen found ignoring the directive. This ruling has dealt a particularly heavy blow to the American Tunaboat Association, who may reach their quota of porpoises two or three months before the tuna season ends and . . ."

Tewfiq switched off the radio with an angry flick and looked at his men.

"Orders," he said at last. "Orders." His voice was heavy with disappointment.

Ibrahim stared at him. "Daoud Hafez tells us to let our porpoise go?" he said incredulously. "After all this?"

"You heard what the woman said: 'Immediate release.' Plus the code words."

"So what are we supposed to do?" asked Sami. "Turn him loose and then quietly disappear and keep our heads down while on Saturday morning our comrades are put in front of Barzuq's firing squad? To hell with that."

"I agree," said Tewfiq simply. "But what can I do? We've been given orders and we've got to stick to them. Daoud Hafez must know something we don't."

"I bet I know what it is," said Wayne. The news of his own impending release had made him almost euphoric. The men looked at him sourly. "I bet I know what this Daoud Hafez wants more than me: Harry Papasian's hundred thousand dollars."

"Son of a whore!" shouted Farid, trying to scramble to his feet and draw his knife at the same time while the other men held him down. "You fat dog! I'll cut your throat for that. I'll . . ." and he raved on, mentioning several other curious and distasteful things he intended doing to Wayne when he had the opportunity.

"You are indeed a dog," Tewfiq observed coldly. "The implication of what you said was not that our leader wants the money more than you, but that he wants it more than the lives of our five comrades. That way he sells each man for a lousy twenty thousand dollars."

Frightened by the sudden fury he had caused, Wayne said sullenly, "So when are you going to free me?"

Tewfiq sprang to his feet and walked briskly over to him. Wayne cowered in a half-crouch on the sand.

"Not yet!" Tewfiq yelled at him. "Not damned yet! Not until I'm good and ready!" He punctuated his words with little kicks, ending up with a boot on Wayne's thigh which gave him an instant "dead leg" and sent him rolling over the floor in agony.

Once more the pain he was in blotted out all exterior events, but by the time Wayne could concentrate on something else, Tewfiq was in earnest conversation with his men, reasoning with them on their best course of action. It seemed to Wayne that they had all been badly shaken by his suggestion that Daoud Hafez had sold them out, for all that it had not been entirely serious. At least Farid seemed to have calmed down and was listening while Tewfiq talked.

"The leader is not expecting us to commit suicide," Tewfiq was saying. "We are valuable and trained guerrillas needed in the struggle. He is not imagining that we will throw our lives away for nothing, and especially not for that piece of dogdung on the floor back there. Orders or no orders, we are not going down to the village while the army is there: it would be stupid and anyway it would put the villagers in needless danger. No, we'll wait until they leave, and then we'll think about ridding ourselves of this brat."

"When we've done that," broke in Ibrahim, "I vote we make for . . ."

"Quiet!" commanded Tewfiq, cutting him off abruptly. "The dog has ears. What he doesn't know about he can't tell. As it is, he knows too much."

"Not very much," countered Sami. "He doesn't know our real names, and he knows less about the organization than the average village policeman."

"Well, let's keep it that way," said Tewfiq.

After a long silence Adil said, "My guess is Daoud Hafez has an alternative and better plan for saving the comrades."

"What?" asked Farid.

"I don't know," admitted Adil, "but I simply can't believe he would abandon them. Not after all this publicity: it would be too great a blow for Seventh January."

The truth was, thought Wayne, nobody had the faintest clue as to what was happening. They were cut off and in the dark as he had suggested they might be, the recipients only of brief coded messages and surprise announcements on the radio. Perhaps it was inevitable, given that kidnappers always had to negotiate from hiding.

Not long afterwards the helicopter took off. Wayne heard its motor start up and crawled forward to watch. It was not yet quite dark. Although the sun had vanished, the western sky was still glowing with the greens and turquoises and vermilions of a desert sunset. The helicopter took off; but instead of heading away it merely began climbing vertically. It went up slowly until it had reached and passed the watchers' own level, and kept on going until Wayne reckoned it was about a thousand feet up. What happened next was so unexpected that at first he could not make out what it was that suddenly detached itself from the machine and, turning slowly, fell through the dusk towards the ground.

Then with a thrill of horror he realized he was watching a man's body. His limbs were flailing, but whether because he was still alive or because the limbs of falling bodies naturally tumbled about, Wayne did not know. About half way down, the man appeared to shed a white sheet, and for an instant of relief Wayne thought it was a parachute opening. But no nylon umbrella mushroomed over him to break his fall, and the man hit the desert less than a hundred meters from the nearest palm trees, his body sending up a little puff of dust while the white material drifted slowly down and settled over a bush nearby. The helicopter turned ponderously and clattered away towards the east. It was not until it was lost against the purple sky and the note of its engine had faded to a hum that anybody spoke.

"Bastards," said Tewfiq between his teeth, and a chorus of swearing broke out. "Well," he went on to Wayne, "now you've seen for yourself how the Government of Zibala treats the people."

Wayne was still half convinced that what he had seen could be explained less horribly than he imagined. In the distance a single figure had broken from the cover of the palm trees and was running towards the body. He suddenly felt sick again.

"Someone fell," he said.

"No they didn't," corrected Tewfiq. "Someone was pushed."

"You mean—deliberately murdered?" It seemed impossible.

"That's right," said Tewfiq. "They threw him out. Some poor rotten peasant they picked up on the way back to the chopper. They took him up, asked him a few questions while threatening to throw him out, and when he had told them all he knew, they put a boot in his back and shoved."

"That wasn't a parachute?" asked Wayne incredulously.

"That was his robe."

"But . . . but if he'd told them what they wanted to know why did they push him out?"

"Because they're the army; they enjoy it. But in any case they were warning the village. They are serious; they'll be back. They don't know for sure that we are here, but they suspect."

"When will they come?" asked Wayne.

"Tomorrow when it gets light. They'll give the villagers the night to think it over."

"I don't understand any of this," Wayne said. "If they thought we were here, why didn't a lot of troops just land in the ordinary way? And why should the villagers know where we are?"

Tewfiq was looking as puzzled as Wayne. "I don't know what your idea of Zibala is, you foreigners, but if you think the Government can send its forces into any part of the country as and when it likes, then you are out of your minds. The Government controls al-Mazar, yes; it controls Marietta, yes. It controls a couple of other large provincial towns, too. It also more or less controls the strip of land between the coast and the capital. The rest of the country—the villages to the south and all the desert areas everywhere—are controlled by local Bedouin families, and always have been. How long is it since the British left Zibala? Thirty years? Not long when you consider that families here have ruled certain areas for five hundred years, father and son, father and son. Where the south of the country and the deserts begin, this stupid Government's jurisdiction ends, believe me. Nobody in a uniform dares travel there."

"But surely with the weapons it has, the army could go in and take the villages for the Government any time it chose?" persisted Wayne.

"It's not that simple," Tewfiq told him. "For a start, a lot of the Bedou are very heavily armed. Remember the 1967 Arab-Israeli War? The desert was littered with abandoned weapons, rifles, artillery, rocket launchers, tanks and armored cars. After the various troops had gone home, the Bedou went around collecting the stuff. To the real desert dweller there are no such things as modern political frontiers: he has far more ancient frontiers of his own, areas which centuries of agreement have recognized as belonging to certain tribes and families. The Zibalan Bedou, like those of neighboring states, simply went in and helped themselves. Would you believe that down there in Bir Huzun, in that tiny little oasis, they have a Russian antiaircraft gun?"

"You're joking," exclaimed Wayne.

"It's there, all right."

"But what on earth do they want it for? Why do they need all these guns and things?"

"Oh," said Tewfiq, "because they're always fighting each other. Just as they have inherited the areas their families control, so they've inherited age-old family feuds. Bedou have the longest memories on earth for feuds. Sometimes in a small village you will find members of one family who won't allow members of another to take a shortcut across their field because of some injury done two hundred years ago but still remembered as if it had happened last week. Sometimes they have great battles, especially now that they are better armed."

"I still don't see what is stopping the Government taking control if it wanted to. The Zibalan army must be able to outgun a lot of Bedou," objected Wayne.

"Sure; if it came to it they probably could," Tewfiq agreed. "But it isn't worth their while. This Government is spread pretty thin as it is: it's a job just holding on to what it already controls. With the sort of weapons it would be facing, the fight could prove costly. The Zibalan army can't afford to lose men, and it certainly can't afford to lose face by taking on a lot of peasants and tribespeople and suffering heavy casualties. So there's a kind of truce. As long as the army and the police don't interfere, the tribal chiefs make sure the people more or less pay their taxes and behave themselves. But once anybody in a uniform comes barging in and trying to upset the authority of a family that has ruled a village for hundreds of years, better watch out."

"I see," said Wayne thoughtfully. He peered out of the cave mouth, but for the third consecutive night there was no moon. The oasis of Bir Huzun was an enigmatic dark stain on the desert below. "What happened just now?"

"I expect that having failed to find us in the south, Barzuq's military commanders decided that we were quite likely to be in these parts. So one of them flew in to open negotiations with the village elders, which is why he left his men by the helicopter. Bir Huzun is controlled by the el Nabi family, so it would have meant dealing with old Sheikh el Nabi himself. The Sheikh is what they call *el rayyis qabila*—the 'president of the tribe' or head of the family. I expect the army man said that there was a political crisis in which the other *rayyis*, President Barzuq, badly needed his help and cooperation. He would have had to offer the Sheikh something in exchange: possibly money or a guarantee of some kind of favor, such as an electricity generating plant for his village. But because Seventh January have a lot of support among the peasants, even in a tiny out-of-the-way place like Bir Huzun, the Sheikh would have asked for a night to think it over."

"You mean the village has known we were here all along?" asked Wayne.

"Of course. Nobody actually knows for certain that we are here in this particular cave, no. But they've got a good idea this is where we probably are. They wouldn't want to know more than that: you've just seen why."

"Then what need had the army to kill that peasant? It doesn't make sense."

"On the contrary," said Tewfiq. "It was a measure of how desperate Barzuq really is. That was the army's way of confirming their suspicions about our presence—not that the

peasant knew for certain, but he would have said he had
heard rumors. More importantly it was a warning to old
Sheikh el Nabi that the army was prepared to antagonize
him or even bomb his village flat if he didn't cooperate.
Barzuq knows it would stir up immense trouble for himself
in this province, but evidently he's prepared to risk it in order
to get you back. Somebody somewhere is twisting his arm
enough to make it hurt quite a bit," he grinned sourly.

"So at dawn tomorrow half the army will be airlifted in to
search all these caves," mused Wayne.

"Nothing of the kind. I've already said that the entire army
could lose itself here for months on end. No, I expect the
same helicopter to come back with the same handful of
troops and the villagers themselves will guide them to this
cave. That will be the deal. Only the villagers know these
caves well enough to be fairly certain of where we are."

"You mean they're selling you out, too."

"No, they aren't," said Tewfiq. "We would have to have
left soon in any case because we haven't much water. The
Sheikh has bought us an entire night in which to make
ourselves scarce."

Wayne thought all this over for a while. He had been taken
aback by this revelation of subtle deals and counterdeals
with which the country seemed to be governed. He had
never suspected that anything like this went on, with the
President having to bargain with Bedouin Sheikhs. It was a
far cry from the world Bernard lived in which seemed to be
run from executive suites or from the dinner table.

"The Sheikh down there knows you know all this?" he
asked Tewfiq finally.

"Of course. We have never met, but the thinking is
obvious. It is how things are here."

"But it won't work out like that," said Wayne.

"Why not?" asked Tewfiq.

"Because I'm being released, of course."

"Of course," agreed Tewfiq, but for a moment it seemed to Wayne that he had forgotten.

Tewfiq got up and set about making tea, it being his turn. The men were still subdued; there was a moody and uneasy tension which was beginning to get on Wayne's nerves. Now he caught Farid looking at him more frequently, glancing up as his hands went on whetting, whetting the blade of his knife on his leather belt which he had taken off, the buckle of which he held between his feet. At ten-fifteen Tewfiq tried the radio again. To everybody's evident surprise there was a repeat of the earlier program about tuna fishing. He turned the set off again and squatted on the floor, staring at the ground beneath him. It was clear that since Wayne's release had not been reported in the last four hours, Daoud Hafez was repeating his order to make sure it was understood. Everybody looked expectantly at Tewfiq.

"I'm going outside," he said shortly, getting to his feet. "Ibrahim will come with me. The others will guard the boy. We will make a move in an hour."

"What sort of a move?" asked Adil.

"Wait and see," snapped his commanding officer, and strode off into the dark tunnel.

Left alone for the first time with Sami, Adil and Farid, Wayne experienced a pang of uneasiness. Yet they would not harm him, he reasoned; not now that Daoud Hafez had given his orders. For about ten minutes the men went into a huddle on the far side of the cave, talking in voices too low and rapid for Wayne to catch. Now and again a glance would be flashed in his direction, and he had the feeling he sometimes had at school when watching teachers whom he knew to be discussing his own fate. Suddenly the group broke up with a burst of laughter which made Wayne's heart race. The men got to their feet and sauntered across the cave. He stood up uncertainly to face them, his back to the sandstone wall. It was practically pitch-dark; the only illumination came from

the familiar cold starlight which seeped in from outside. In it
the men's faces were menacing pale blotches.

"We have a score to settle, Puppy," said Adil.

"What score?" demanded Wayne, his voice high with
nervousness.

"The you and the us," said Adil enigmatically. "Now it's
us." He took a step forward.

Wayne bent swiftly down, still keeping his eyes on the
man, and found a lump of rock on the floor with one hand.
He raised it menacingly. "You stay away from me!" he
shouted. The sound of his own voice mysteriously increased
his panic. He could actually feel his hair bristling.

Farid, who still held his belt dangling from one hand,
stepped casually forward and flicked it out. The leather
curled with a stinging crack across Wayne's cheek, splitting
the skin and doubling him over with his hands pressed to his
face. The rock lay where it had fallen. Adil reached forward
and, grasping the boy by his hair, lugged him away from the
cave wall and threw him sprawling on the floor.

Instinct told Wayne that he was fighting for his life. He
rolled over and flung a double handful of sand and gravel
into the faces which hung leeringly over him. They retreated
momentarily with cries of pain and anger, wiping their eyes.
Then, more warily, the three surrounded him in the half
crouches of men accustomed to hand-to-hand fighting. A
terrible weariness overcame Wayne. He knew he could not
hope to defend himself. For a grotesque instant he found
himself in imagination standing to one side, looking on as if
none of it concerned him. He saw his hated physical self, a
fat and bleeding boy thinking about taking on three grown
men with guerrilla training. Then he was back inside his
body again, filled with resignation. He noticed inconsequen-
tially that all three men had now taken off their belts.

"Me first," said Farid, who held his knife loosely in one
hand. "We swore an oath."

Adil stepped forward and suddenly grabbed both

Wayne's ears. The boy found himself wrenched to the ground like a wounded steer. A knee in the small of his back pinned him immovably to the cave floor. A foul waft of breath engulfed his head. He tried to call Tewfiq's name, but all that came from his squeezed lungs was a gasp.

"Now, Puppy," said Farid's voice from close by his ear.

Chapter 7

On Thursday morning the American School of al-Mazar conducted—as it had the two previous mornings—special nondenominational prayers for Wayne. The Chaplain was a pretty nondenominational sort of man. He made a point of not caring whether God was Roman Catholic, Presbyterian, Moslem, Buddhist, Russian Orthodox or Jewish—although as yet no foreign company had committed the indiscretion of sending a practicing Jewish executive to Zibala. The Chaplain would refer equally happily—depending on whom he was addressing—to "Allah-the-Great" or to "the One" or simply to "Him Up There." Now, on this Thursday morning, he asked his flock to close its eyes and reach out to ask the Spirit of the Universe to protect the soul of Wayne Bulkeley and restore him to his parents and friends.

Many of the older members of his flock could barely have kept their eyes open in any case. They were recovering, as they did every morning, from the aftereffects of the previous night's excesses. The sons and daughters of Zibala's foreign community were mightily bored. Since they had no desire to join in with the activities their parents had devised—the Bridge Club, the Scottish Country Dancing Club, the Grand Old Raised Elbow Club and the rest—they gave endless parties for themselves while their parents were out. Nearly every night the luxuriously appointed villas in al-Mazar's

residential community were full of teen-agers helping
themselves to their fathers' duty-free Scotch and duty-free
stereo music systems. This was a start.

What really made these parties go, however, was the
excellent quality of the drugs which could easily be bought
in the right quarter of the city. Bernard's friend Damian was
not alone in his discovery of the wicked effects of Zibalan
hash; the kids arrived at school next morning with their eyes
like currants in a bun, stoned, zonked, bombed out.

Bernard stood at the back of the students' assembly hall
listening to the prayers. Aloof, impassive, he was not
recovering from any hangover. He was very sober and very
miserable. He did not believe in God, he believed in
diplomacy; he therefore considered it a supreme waste of
time praying for Wayne. And yet he alone out of the three
hundred-odd people in the hall had spent sleepless nights on
his friend's behalf. He had been surprised by how much he
found himself caring that Wayne should be all right. Viewed
objectively, the kidnapping was the most exciting thing to
have happened to the American School since the visit by two
"Governors" who had been revealed as Narcotics Bureau
investigators. In school, people talked of nothing else.
Classes were interrupted for news bulletins; a collection was
taken for an enormous bouquet of flowers for Wayne's
parents which, Bernard considered, looked painfully like a
wreath. There was not a student in the school who had not
known Wayne's distinctive figure by sight, at least, and in a
bid for reflected glory and involvement many of them were
pretending they were his friends. This annoyed Bernard
very much; for while he could truthfully say he was Wayne's
only real friend at the school, he was suddenly forced to
wonder exactly what it was he was claiming to which the
others had no right.

As the hours and now days had dragged by without a word
from either Wayne or the kidnappers, Bernard had become
more deeply sunk in gloom. The Wednesday deadline had

passed more than twenty hours ago and there was still no news of whether the Seventh January had carried out their hideous promise to mutilate Wayne. But almost worse was the knowledge that his own father's assured predictions had been proved false.

Bernard had an almost religious belief in his father's rightness in such matters, and not without reason. He had grown up as M. Levesque had risen from being First Secretary Political at the Embassy in Istanbul, via Junior Ambassador in Afghanistan and Baghdad, to Ambassador in the important post of Zibala. Ambassador Levesque was still only forty-five, and he had risen that far that quickly by being right more often than his contemporaries. Now, however, it seemed he was wrong. Somewhere there was an error—whether in information or diagnosis. Either Ambassador Levesque knew enough to be certain that President Barzuq would have to back down, or he was trying to cheer his son up, or he didn't know enough and was wrong. Bernard was baffled and upset.

He became aware that the prayers were over and the students were breaking up and drifting away to their classes. The Chaplain bore down on him, smiling encouragingly. However, instead of grasping his shoulder manfully as Bernard feared he might, the man merely came to an awkward stop in front of him.

"Uh, I know you're not a believer yourself, Bernard," he began. "But I do think our prayers can be a powerful force for good at a time like this. I know Wayne is a particular friend of yours, and I am sure we can help him by driving out evil with our love."

Bernard was uncertain whether the Chaplain was chiding him for ostentatiously refusing to join in the prayers or merely explaining what the idea behind them was.

"Thank you," he said stiffly. Then he added, "It's all a lot of bullshit anyway."

The Chaplain grinned delightedly. This was familiar territory to him.

"Well then," he said, "let's hope the bullshit *works*." He winked at Bernard and strode off.

"I can't understand it," Harry Papasian was saying for the hundredth time. With the time lag it was the middle of the night in Manhattan but he would not leave his office on top of the MOPEC building. With the exception of his aide Dan all his personal staff had been dismissed hours ago. Now he strode up and down the Kashmiri carpets in his office, a glass of his favorite French mineral water in one pudgy hand.

"I can't understand it, Dan," he said again. Dan, sitting behind him with a note pad and poised ballpoint raised his eyes to the ceiling. "Are you quite sure about that telex from Jim? It *is* from Jim Cathcart in Amman?" he added foolishly.

"Quite sure, Mr. Papasian. I'll read it again if you like. It says . . ." Dan found a slip of paper tucked into his notebook—

OFFER ONEFIFTY GRAND GRATEFULLY ACCEPTED PIRATE CHIEF WHO CLAIMS MESSAGE TO TEAM WILL SECURE RELEASE WITHIN THREE HOURS STOP WE HAVE MAN STANDING BY FOR TRADEOFF STOP NO MONEY CHANGES HANDS UNTIL GOODS PRESENT AND VOUCHED INTACT STOP JIM STOP MESSAGE ENDS

That's it, Mr. Papasian."

"H'm. It was coded, of course. I suppose there couldn't have been any mistake in the decipherment?"

"Hardly," said Dan. "If they had gotten one thing wrong the whole lot would be gibberish. Besides, have you ever known Communications to louse things up?"

"So where's the kid?" Harry Papasian opened his arms, slopping water on the carpet as he wheeled to face the almost empty room. " 'Three hours,' he says. Three hours, three hours. How long since we got that telex?"

"It was timed at six o'clock last night in Amman. That's a little over twelve hours ago."

"Twelve hours, for Heaven's sake. What the hell's going on? Is there no news at all from anyone?"

"Not a peep. Our Embassy in Zibala says there has been nothing on the local radio and the British BBC have nothing, either."

"Well, there's been a foul-up somewhere. Perhaps Daoud Hafez can't get in touch with his gang. I thought he was supposed to be quite competent as things go. I hope they didn't start carving that kid up before the message got through . . . Anyway"— Harry Papasian looked on the bright side— "I told you, didn't I? Remember what I said? I said I thought Hafez was hooked and now we know he was. I know men like Hafez: I eat them for breakfast. He wants money, it's that simple."

"For himself, you mean?" asked Dan.

"For himself, for his Seventh January thing, who knows? Maybe the guy is an idealist after all. Whatever the reason, right now he wants the cash more than he wants the kid. Who cares why? Perhaps he's got something better lined up. Just so long as it's not another MOPEC employee I'm not bothered," said Harry Papasian. "If . . ." He broke off as the telephone rang, grabbed the receiver and said "Papasian." He listened for a moment, grunted a few times and then hung up.

"Communications," he said to Dan. "Jim Cathcart has come through to say he has still heard nothing and should he try to get in touch with Hafez again. Says he's worried. He's not the only one."

"Do you think it would help if he contacted Hafez?" Dan asked.

"No, I do not," his boss told him shortly. "The offer has been made and has been accepted. There's nothing to add and no further negotiating to be done. It's up to Hafez now.

But if we still haven't heard by"—he glanced at his watch—
"say six A.M., then I'll get Jim to cancel the offer. It's as simple
as that."

"What happens to the kid if you do?"

Harry Papasian shrugged. "What indeed?" he said.

In al-Mazar it was midmorning and U.S. Ambassador Vance
Deedle had been summoned to President Barzuq's office. He
arrived in the Embassy's stately black Lincoln, the Stars and
Stripes snapping stiffly from its little chrome rod, looking
every inch the representative of a world power calling on the
president of a troublesome but minor country whom he was
regretfully going to have to start bullying.

The Ambassador certainly felt like bullying someone: the
strain of the last few days had been considerable. His
Residence had been completely taken over by the Bulkeleys
and their nervous tension. They never seemed to sleep, they
never seemed to eat. The father spent his time smacking a fist
into his palm, muttering "sonofabitch," or meditating with
some ghastly Buddhist that MOPEC had imported. Mrs., on
the other hand, kept wondering if they were feeding her boy
properly. To judge from a snapshot of Wayne Jr. she had
shown him, that Ambassador doubted whether more food
was what he needed.

All this was wearying. But on top of it, right at the moment
he had decided to demand an audience with Barzuq and slap
down an Official Protest, a curt note had arrived from
Barzuq summoning him instead. Had he not felt so slowed
down by these Bulkeleys, the Ambassador thought crossly,
he would never have let Barzuq take the initiative. He was
not in the best mood as he bowed formally in the President's
hideous apricot-and-purple reception room.

"Mr. Ambassador," said the Zibalan when the formalities
were over. "I have asked you here to register the strongest
possible protest at the way in which your country is
conducting itself. I may say that we in Zibala have been

deeply shocked—and I myself extremely disappointed—at the part played by the United States in the present difficult affair. I must therefore ask that you cease forthwith from this policy, otherwise I am afraid steps must be taken which may compromise the hitherto friendly relations of our two countries." He paused for breath.

"Mr. President," said the Ambassador, "I am afraid you must be misinformed. I can promise you that the United States has played practically no part—disreputable or otherwise—in this lamentable business. As I am sure you know, although this concerns the kidnapping of a U.S. citizen, our policy is to rely on the agencies for law and order in the host country, giving advice or help only when asked to do so. In short," said Ambassador Deedle, "we have done nothing but sit around and wait for your people to come up with something."

Ismail Barzuq turned and walked over to a glass-topped table and picked up a scrap of paper. "Is that so?" he said frostily. "Then how do you explain that our Intelligence informs us the President of MOPEC, Harold Papasian, is still negotiating directly with Daoud Hafez? In fact, we learn that he has now increased his offer to one hundred and fifty thousand dollars for the boy's release. The United States," he said triumphantly, "does not consider doing deals with international terrorist organizations to be disreputable?"

"Damn Papasian" was the Ambassador's first thought. "Somebody's head is going to roll for this" was his second. Aloud he said: "Mr. President, what you have just said amounts to a grave charge laid against the integrity of the country I represent. It is a charge I have no hesitation in refuting utterly and categorically. I am assured that the news which the BBC broadcast alleging an original offer of one hundred thousand dollars was completely false. My State Department says that no such offer was ever made and that they do not know where the story originated. Now you claim that a second offer has been made. I hate to say it, but I fear your Intelligence service has made a mistake. Presumably its sources were as badly misinformed as were the BBC."

Ismail Barzuq reached into his pocket and came out with another piece of paper. "You might think so," he agreed, "if it were not for this." And he handed the stunned Ambassador a copy of Harry Papasian's cable to Jim Cathcart in Amman, flawlessly deciphered into its original wording.

"Mr. President," said Ambassador Deedle stiffly, "I beg leave of you to go and consult my State Department. Personally, I think we have both been hoaxed . . ."

"You think this telex is a fake?" interrupted Barzuq.

"I'm not saying it's a fake," said the Ambassador doggedly. "All I am saying is that I think we are being hoaxed. I do not for one moment believe that your accusations have a grain of truth in them; but I would like to say that if they were found to stand up then I personally would be as profoundly shocked as you. Good day, Mr. President." And with that Vance Deedle walked out of the room, icy with composure.

Once back in his own office at the Embassy, however, the ice broke. "Get me State Department!" he roared to his Communications clerk. "I want that man Papasian hanged from the top of his MOPEC building by his own entrails," he informed his galvanized staff. "I want it done slowly, but I want it started NOW!"

Later in the day when he had confirmed that Barzuq was perfectly correct, he debated sending a Note of Apology. He was still furious, but his rage had subsided from a blaze to a smoulder. Typical businessman, thought the Ambassador of Harry Papasian, just typical. You bend over backwards to ease their multimillion-dollar deals through for the sake of the economy, they get nicely rich, thank you, and then they come trampling all over delicate diplomatic territory as if they owned the world. Well, we'll cook *his* goose for him . . . And as for Barzuq's Note of Apology, he could not bring himself to write it yet.

"The old bastard can wait a bit," he confided to an

elaborate glass paperweight on his desk top. "He's kept us
hanging around before now; he can damn well wait for his
apology."

He was less decided about whether to tell the Bulkeleys.
Officially, the affair of MOPEC's offer was classified
information; but since the President of Zibala already knew
about it, the whole world would also know the entire story
shortly. On the other hand he did not want to upset the
Bulkeleys by pointing out that since Harry Papasian was still
muscling in on the negotiations anything might happen.
Their son was rapidly becoming a mere pawn in the middle
of a three-way fight between Zibala, MOPEC and the
United States.

When he saw Mrs. Bulkeley at lunch, the Ambassador
nearly did tell her out of a sense of duty which urged him to
keep an anxious mother fully informed. But the moment she
asked him if he thought the terrorists were giving Wayne any
lunch, he decided that he was not going to tell her. Serve her
right. And when she came up with her next question—
positively the stupidest that anyone had asked him in the last
week—he was quite sure he wasn't. She looked thoughtfully
at the Ambassador and asked: "Has anybody here stopped to
wonder who these prisoners are that they're going to shoot,
and what they're supposed to have done? Why can't they be
freed?"

Chapter 8

ALMOST AS SOON as it had so crushingly descended, the weight of the knee lifted off Wayne's back. Suddenly free to move, he rolled weakly over and in the dimness of the cave saw the men standing around awkwardly as Tewfiq faced them. He never said a word but merely stared very hard at Adil and Farid until they walked off in silence by themselves. Then he said:

"We have a visitor."

Getting weakly to his feet, seemingly unhurt except for his whipped face, Wayne found a stranger standing between Tewfiq and Ibrahim.

"Who's this?" he asked.

"We came back at exactly the right moment, I should say," Tewfiq remarked, looking him over. "This?" he asked, suddenly seeming to have heard Wayne's question. "This is Ahmed, from Bir Huzun. He came up to the village to find us. We found him instead." Wayne noticed that the man was holding his left wrist as if it hurt him. "There was a misunderstanding in the darkness, but no harm done. You"—he broke off and addressed Sami—"will go and tell your friends Adil and Farid to make us some tea and get a move on." He slapped the magazine of the gun slung over one shoulder. "Come, we'll sit down." He led the way over to the cave mouth, and they sat looking down at the endless black wasteland beneath.

Wayne noticed that Ahmed was staring at him with considerable curiosity, as he might at anybody he had heard mentioned regularly on the radio.

"What's happening?" Wayne asked in Arabic. Ahmed's stare became even wider.

"I was right," said Tewfiq. "It all happened just as I told you. The army came to negotiate with Sheikh el Nabi, and they're coming back tomorrow."

"Oh," said Wayne. "So I suppose you'll leave me in the village for when they arrive?"

"Perhaps," said Tewfiq noncommittally. Wayne did not at all like the offhand tone; surely he was not going to remain their prisoner when their leader had repeated his own order that he should be freed? "The man they threw out of the helicopter," Tewfiq interrupted his fears. "That was Ahmed's father."

It was Wayne's turn to stare at Ahmed with sudden shock. For the first time he saw a boy not much older than himself.

"I'm very sorry," he said inadequately, feeling almost as if it had been his own fault.

"It was the will of Allah," replied the boy, his eyes glistening in the starlight.

"It was the will of the army commander, you mean," Wayne corrected him angrily.

"The will of the army commander was the will of Allah," said Tewfiq gently. "That too was willed. Ahmed's father led a good life. His death will not go unavenged."

Wayne could well believe it. If what Tewfiq had told him was true, it was probably the beginning of a centuries-long feud which would drag on from one generation to the next, punctuated by squalid acts of violence. For a brief, flaring instant Wayne had an insight of an unbroken chain of pointless suffering and enmity stretching down the years well past his own death, a chain whose first link he was by reason of a chance and unwilling involvement with foreign people in a foreign land.

They drank the tea in silence, after which Ahmed, with a word of thanks, got up and left. Tewfiq kissed him on both cheeks and escorted him away to the back of the cave. When he reappeared, he said to his men:

"We'll go now. I have made a decision and that is we fight on. We keep Wayne"—he used the name for the first time—"because I still believe that he remains our only hope for buying the lives of our comrades on Saturday morning. It is possible our leader has plans of his own for freeing them, but one of them is my friend and I cannot take the risk. My friendship makes that impossible. I propose that we move overnight to another place where we can hide safely and repeat our demands. This is against Daoud Hafez's orders. I will not force you to go against his command, so if any of you don't wish to go on with me leave your weapons here and go your own way to continue the struggle elsewhere. There will be no dishonor. Who wants to leave us?"

There was a brief silence.

"Me," said Wayne. To his surprise the men all broke into laughter. Tewfiq clapped him on the back.

"That's what we've needed all along," he said. "A comedian. We haven't had enough laughs. Right, comrades. Thank you all for your friendship and loyalty. We fight on."

"I stay on one condition," said a voice. It was Adil, injecting his own special brand of chill into the proceedings.

"What's that?" Tewfiq asked him.

"That we cut off one of this dog's toes *right now* so that Barzuq can see it on his breakfast table. We've sat around and we've sat around in this damned cave like a colony of drugged bats. Now it's time to show Barzuq that we mean business. Time is running short. Well, do we cut or do I go?"

"You go," said Tewfiq quietly.

"Uh?" Adil was plainly taken aback.

"I have a better idea. We allow him to make a tape recording to his parents or to the American Ambassador. He will make an eloquent plea because he knows that he's going to die if our comrades die. I have sworn this and I will shoot him myself with this gun—" He tapped the barrel of his weapon. "Some time on Thursday they will get that cassette, and the Ambassador will at once get his State Department's permission to use big guns. Then if by Friday Barzuq hasn't capitulated, we will start trimming the boy's feet. As a special treat, Adil, you may do the knife work."

There was a pause while Adil thought this over. At length he said reluctantly:

"Okay, I'll stay until Friday. But after then"—he looked significantly around, his knife point travelling from one member of the group to the next—"no more deals. Only business." He put the knife away with a flourish.

The journey down from the cave was far easier than the original ascent had been. On Tewfiq's orders they left the jerry cans with what remained of the water, the Primus stove and tea-making equipment. They took only their weapons, the flashlights and the radio. To Wayne's surprise they even abandoned the Land Rover, passing its place of concealment without a pause.

Soon they had reached the foot of the cliff and were trudging across the stony desert towards where the thick stand of shaggy palms ahead marked the edge of the oasis of Bir Huzun. As they entered the deep gloom beneath the trees through whose foliage the starlight could barely penetrate, they were joined by a dark and silent figure. Wayne recognized Ahmed. The youth led the way among the tree trunks until they came to the black outline of a small flat-roofed house. There was a smell of wood smoke. Somewhere nearby a dog barked once and a few chickens clucked softly, their sleep disturbed. A door creaked open; a gentle yellow glow spilled out, and Wayne felt a propelling hand push him gently but firmly over the threshold.

The room inside was small and bare, with very little in the

way of decoration. On the wall opposite the door hung a single sepia photograph of a young man with a large black moustache, presumably Ahmed's father in his youth. Along the left-hand wall was a low bed, and on it lay the body of a dead old man. Beside the bed sat an *imam* reading aloud from the Qur'an. He held the book up high to catch the light of the single lamp on the table beside him. From one wrist dangled a string of prayer beads, an Islamic rosary. The light gleamed dully on an ancient-looking shotgun with twin hammers curling like swans' necks hanging on the wall above the bed.

"*Abui*," said Ahmed quietly. "My father."

The men approached the bed, murmuring phrases in Arabic which might have been the ritual salutations and commiserations for such moments or else appropriate quotations from the Qur'an. A rough cotton sheet had been pulled up under the dead man's chin, and from the irregular lumpiness beneath it and the large brown stains of dried blood Wayne could guess at the appalling nature of the injuries. He looked away in horror, but even so there was a part of him functioning with a clinical detachment. How strange, he thought, that a man should fall a thousand feet and burst on stony desert and yet have a face that seemed entirely untouched by anything but age.

After a bit Ahmed led Tewfiq and Wayne through a door into a second room roughly the size of the first. He produced a box of matches, and another oil lamp bloomed slowly into orange light. Relieved to be in a different room but still very uncomfortable, Wayne realized he was less like a kidnap victim at the mercy of Arab terrorists than a foreign guest who had by chance been invited into the home of some peasant whom, unwittingly and quite by accident, he had caused a great injury. And for the second time he experienced a brief, intense mental image of himself as being irrevocably linked with several alien lives. He had never wanted it, but it had happened. He glanced back at the closed, elderly face of the man who lay on the bed, but felt only a conventional kind of sadness. Behind that was the feeling that everything which had happened to him in the last few days had been grotesquely unfair. He had been injured and starved and terrified without having deserved any of it, and now it seemed that he was at least partly answerable for the death of a man. Nothing in his family or at school had prepared him for this. Without warning the comfortably undramatic production of his life had been recast, and he had suddenly found himself pitchforked into a new role in a melodrama played without rehearsal and entirely by foreigners. What had he to do with these people?

Ahmed closed the door gently and the low chanting of the *imam* became inaudible. Tewfiq began talking softly and urgently to him, reaching into his top pocket as he did so. A thick roll of money changed hands. Wayne thought he caught the words for "truck" and "travel" but could not be sure. Ahmed reached up to a shelf and took down a Japanese combination radio and cassette recorder.

"*Fi* cassette?" Tewfiq asked.

"*Fi. Guwwa.*" Ahmed pressed a button and a cassette popped out.

"We will have to take it," said Tewfiq. He offered Ahmed another banknote.

"It doesn't matter," said the youth, pushing Tewfiq's hand away.

"*Mutshakkir.*"

Ahmed opened the back door, peered out and slipped through. The door closed behind him.

"He's gone to fix up some transport for us," Tewfiq told Wayne. "Meanwhile, you've also got a job to do." He hefted the tape recorder in one hand. "You're going to record a message for your mummy and your daddy and the nice American Ambassador. Oh, yes, your mother's from England, isn't she? I suppose that means you have two nationalities. Well, the British Ambassador, too."

"A different message for each one?"

"Just the one. We'll do the marketing and distribution." Tewfiq might have been discussing the sales of a popular record. "They will all be listening to your voice by lunchtime."

"Oh," said Wayne, half pleased by the idea of any sort of communication with his former life and half fearful of how to do it. "What am I going to say?"

"Really, you're telling them that you're alive and well but that you soon won't be unless Barzuq releases those men and flies them out of the country. Obviously, you are not allowed to describe us or our surroundings. You may think," said Tewfiq, "that because we are not behaving like wild beasts your life is no longer in any danger. You are quite wrong. If it would buy the lives of our friends, I would cut your throat here and now." Wayne realized the man was perfectly sincere. "If you need any convincing, I shall leave you alone with Farid for just five minutes. I think that would be enough."

"More than," agreed Wayne. "Please don't do that; there's no need."

"I didn't think there would be," said Tewfiq drily. He put the tape recorder down on a bench. "Start talking at the machine; the microphone's built in."

Feeling absurd and self-conscious, Wayne sat and faced the machine. The whole thing was mad, sitting in the middle of the desert in a house with a dead man in it, recording a message to his parents to plead for his life. "Hello," he began stupidly. "Er . . . this is Wayne. I'm all right really . . ." he caught Tewfiq's eye. "They're looking after me and treating me well. But you've got to believe what they say, Dad. They're not fooling. You must get the President to release the five prisoners before Saturday. Tewfiq . . ."

Click! went the recorder. "Stupid," remarked Tewfiq. He wound back the tape an inch or two to the end of Wayne's previous sentence. "Now try again."

"Er . . . They've promised to kill me if the men aren't freed and flown out of the country, and they really mean it. I know they do. The prisoners are their friends, and they say they have nothing more to lose." He saw Tewfiq nodding and stopped. Tewfiq switched off the machine.

"You're doing fine. But can't you cry and do that 'Mummy Mummy, Daddy Daddy' bit they have in American films?"

"No," said Wayne, "not really. I . . . " He shrugged. "I don't really feel it—it's all too unreal."

"I think I'd better fetch Farid."

"Oh no, no, please not," Wayne began, but Tewfiq stood up nevertheless. "No," Wayne begged him. Tewfiq slapped him backhandedly across the face, reopening the split in his cheek from Farid's belt. Wayne gasped and felt the blood beginning to run again. His hands went to his face, and Tewfiq hit him lightly in the stomach, doubling him up with a groan. "Stop," gasped the boy. "I'll do it, damn you, anything you say. Just leave me alone. I'm sick of the things you keep doing to me. I just want to be the hell out of here and go home." And despite himself, Wayne burst into tears.

Tewfiq watched him in some amusement for a few seconds.

"Lovely," he remarked, clicking off the recorder.

"You recorded that?" Wayne asked him, gulping and sniffing.

"Sure. I turned it on when you weren't looking just after I threatened to fetch Farid. It's good stuff. That'll convince your dear mother."

"You're a real bastard, aren't you?" Wayne said, amazement drying his tears.

"So would you be if they were putting someone you love in front of a firing squad, believe me."

Wayne thought of Bernard listening to the tape, then his parents. He was suddenly overcome with pity, not all of it for himself.

"We want an ending," Tewfiq said. "I want you to say that

to save your life Barzuq has to do it in two stages. Firstly, he has to take our five comrades to Marietta Airport and not al-Mazar Airport. When we know they are there—perhaps he'll televise it—we will negotiate the next stage which will involve us all getting on a plane together. Okay?"

Wayne repeated the information. When he had finished, he added in a blurt: "Please do something quickly," and ended "love Wayne" as if he had been writing a letter. Tewfiq rewound the tape and ran it through again, Wayne listening in misery and embarrassment.

"It's good," cried Tewfiq at the end. He checked the remainder of the tape on both sides for any recordings which might compromise Ahmed, then put the cassette back in its plastic case. As if on cue, Ahmed himself came through the door.

"Okay," he said, "it's all fixed. You're going to"—he glanced at Wayne—"where you wanted." He looked back at Wayne a second time, noting the fresh blood on his cheek. "Have you finished?"

"Yes," said Tewfiq. He stood up and put the tape in his pocket. "*Yallah*, let's move."

They left the house by the back door. Outside under the trees it was cold and dark and very still. Not a palm frond rustled. Ahmed led the way until they were standing between two dark bulks which smelled strongly of diesel fuel.

"Ibrahim, the boy and I will take this one," said Tewfiq, slapping a huge rear tire as if it had been the haunch of a beast of burden. "Sami, Farid and Adil go in the other. Okay?"

With some difficulty Wayne climbed up over the high tailboard and practically fell into the truck. The back was piled high with greenery of sorts.

"Vegetables," Tewfiq said, joining him. "Every week these drivers do a run to Dabbah with vegetables they grow here in Bir Huzun. This week we're going too."

Wayne was surprised, "I didn't know there were any roads from here."

"There aren't. Who needs roads when the desert's so flat? The drivers know the way. They were born here." Tewfiq pushed him over a mountain of greenstuff to the cab end of the truck where there were no vegetables but a large panel of flat wickerwork supported by boxes so as to allow a space of about two feet between it and the floor. "Get in under there." Tewfiq indicated a space.

Wayne crawled in and found he was lying on some sacking which smelled strongly of old cheese. "This is going to be awful," he muttered half aloud. He heard Tewfiq and Ibrahim sliding in, one on either side of him, and then someone began throwing vegetables on top of the wickerwork. Dried mud and sand rained down onto Wayne, together with fragments of leaf and root. Bit by bit the stars were blotted out until he lay in a total darkness which smelled of fresh cabbages and cheese, listening to the distant thuds of yet more vegetables being piled onto the layer overhead. The cabbage leaves squeaked beneath the weight.

"Okay?" came Tewfiq's voice from close by.

"*Meshi*," answered Ibrahim.

"How long is this going to last?" Wayne wanted to know.

"About four hours."

"But we'll suffocate. We haven't enough air for four minutes."

"Shut up," said Tewfiq irritably. "I've never known anybody make such a fuss. I don't know why you aren't more grateful to us."

At first Wayne was speechless. "What the hell have I got to be grateful to you about?" he demanded at length. He squirmed around on the cheesy rags, grazing his shoulder on a protruding stub of wicker. The darkness and confinement of his tiny cell were oppressive.

"We have at least got you out of that disgusting life you

were leading. Too much food and too many fools. You're all a lot of rich zombies."

"What do you mean, too many fools?" demanded Wayne.

"You're surrounded by them," came the reply from the darkness. "Don't forget we watched your precious friend Levesque for long enough."

"If you think Bernard's a fool, you're making a big mistake."

Tewfiq laughed. "I don't think, I *know* he is. Conceited little man about town with his suits and cologne. He's what the French call *fils à papa*. Do you know the expression?" Wayne lay silent in the dark.

"He thinks because his father is some crummy little Ambassador that he owns the world. How old is he? Not quite sixteen, but he thinks because he has met a few presidents and has been to parties with the flotsam of capitalist society which drifts in and out of the 'People' column of *Time* magazine that he knows how the world works."

"That isn't true," cried Wayne, distressed. "Bernard isn't like that at all. He can't help having moved in important circles because his father's important."

"His father," went on Tewfiq imperturbably, "is a little heap of bat's excrement. M. Levesque is not, will never be, and has never been of the least importance. Ambassador of Quebec!" he spat contemptuously. "Who the hell is the Ambassador of Quebec? What's Quebec? A republic of absolutely no international significance. What do you think he knows? Do you imagine any of the world powers chat to Quebec about what they're doing? You'd learn more about politics by bugging your own father's telephone than you would by listening to Ambassador Levesque. Young Bernard is a vain and conceited product of an overpaid and useless society, and it's a damn good job for him that we got you instead because by now I should have cut his throat and gone home, comrades or no comrades."

Over the last few days Wayne had grown accustomed to
Tewfiq's impassioned outbursts. He had listened to them
partly because he had little option but also because he was
interested. Tewfiq had told him things he had never known
and had left him thinking about things he had never wanted
to think about. But this latest tirade left him baffled and
uneasy. He supposed people did not become guerrillas and
join groups like Seventh January unless they were em-
bittered in some way; but this personal attack on his friend
was quite unexpected. He did not know what to think.
Instead, he said: "I wish we'd go soon and get this whole
thing over," and as if in answer to this wish, the engine of the
truck started with a roar, the floor drumming to its vibrations
beneath his head.

Suddenly, the driver let the clutch in and they lurched off.
Above the noise of the engine he heard the faint sound of the
second truck starting, and then nothing was audible except
the total noise of the diesel motor. It seemed to fill the space
beneath the cabbages like a physical body, further
squeezing Wayne until he lay like a seed, curled up for self-
protection and slammed up and down against the floor.

The journey became a waking dream. Wayne never knew
whether he fell completely asleep or was continually
bounced between sleep and agonized wakefulness. Fitful
images came to him: of an overnight train journey across
Europe he had once made with his mother when he had
woken several times with a start in his *couchette* and,
peeping blearily from behind the curtain, had each time
found the train standing in complete silence at a deserted
platform lit by cold mercury-vapor lamps. Next he was
plunged into a nightmare in which he and Bernard had
somehow turned into dice being rolled around in an
enormous shaker. "I shall be a six," Bernard cried each time
they collided, "but there will be no dishonor if you are not."
And finally, of being flown by a gigantic Arab in a helicopter
to a massage parlor in a Hilton Hotel where he was

strapped into a machine designed to vibrate the fat off overweight tourists. "There will be no charge," the Arab kept saying. "You are doing us a favor. We cannot accept money. There will be no charge."

The jolting had stopped; the roar of the engine had subsided to a slow idle. Faint voices sounded from outside.

"Can you hear me?" came Tewfiq's voice softly.

"Yes," said Wayne.

"Good. I want you to know I have my gun pointed at your stomach. If you make any attempt to attract attention, I shall simply pull the trigger."

"All right," said Wayne. Then, as an afterthought, "Where are we?"

"About three-quarters of the way. This'll be a police check post. I hope for all our sakes they are half asleep as usual." A police post, thought Wayne to himself. And then, as if he had heard the thought, Tewfiq added: "They control the roads around here, nothing else."

But evidently the driver had aroused no suspicion, for he revved the engine, let in the clutch and they were off once more.

"Alhamdulillah!" shouted Ibrahim next to his ear. With a start Wayne realized he had forgotten the man's existence.

"Alhamdulillah!" replied Tewfiq. Suddenly Wayne was aware of something nudging his thigh. He was surprised to find Tewfiq's hand thrusting something into his.

"From Ahmed!" came Tewfiq's shout.

They were peppermit lumps, three of them. Wayne lay there in the jolting darkness and thought he had never tasted anything so good. The sweetness was almost unbearable, and the flavor of mint seemed to rise in a cloud around him and engulf him, blotting out the sour stink of vegetables, cheese and diesel fumes. Wayne could feel himself expanding to contain such sweetness, his spirits rising until he almost floated, content to be carried by armed men to an unknown destination and perhaps to his death. That something as small as a mint lump could so alter the circumstances of living came to him as a complete revelation.

Eventually the journey ended. For a quarter of an hour the truck had bumped along what must have been an unmade track after turning off the comparative comfort of an asphalt surface. The note of its engine changed, and the floor took on a slight slope as they climbed a gentle incline. Then after one or two further lurches, the truck stopped and the engine was switched off. An incredible silence fell. The sudden quiet was so soft it was like being in a velvet cocoon. Then the cab door creaked open, and the vehicle rocked slightly as feet clambered about on the cargo overhead. There were sounds of labor and suddenly a fragment of sky the color of tarnished silver appeared. Bit by bit more sky came into view, and then their wicker roof was lifted off, and hands reached down to help them up. Soon Wayne found himself standing beside the truck cramped and shivering in the dawn cold. The sun had not yet risen, but there was enough light to show his surroundings.

They were on top of a small hill. Next to him rose a high stone wall, and Wayne saw that it belonged to a building which at first sight he took to be a castle. It reminded him of the desert forts in films about the French Foreign Legion, except that they no longer seemed to be in the desert proper. The hillside sloped away, covered with an extensive grove of short trees, which might have been olives or oranges or even figs. In the distance—how far it was impossible to judge in this light—Wayne saw that the hillside ended in the smoothest, most featureless desert he had ever seen, before he realized that he was looking at the sea.

By this time they had been joined by the rest of the group from the second truck, Adil and Farid brushing mud and sand out of their hair and dusting off their weapons. The two drivers were evidently anxious to be off. Tewfiq took them aside and spoke briefly to them, before handing one of them the cassette which Wayne had recorded. They were both identically dressed in robes with lengths of some pale material wrapped around their heads. They were both young men, Wayne noticed. One had a distinctively fleshy nose, while the other who took the cassette lacked two fingers from his right hand. They saluted Tewfiq and then climbed back into their cabs. Without a backward glance they started their engines, turned around and trundled away down the hill.

"Inside, everyone," Tewfiq ordered, and indicated a narrow door in the wall on the far side of a dry and shallow moat. This, Wayne noticed as they crossed, was full of the usual rubbish of dried excrement, shreds of newspaper, old condensed milk tins and unidentifiable piles of vegetable matter. With Farid's gun in his back he hurried in through the door.

Inside he found that the *Beau Geste* appearance of the fort's exterior was maintained. He was in a large enclosure, roughly square, contained by the high walls. On one side was the main house, which extended right to the top of the wall. Against the other three sides were low stables and outhouses. In the middle was a large sandy patch in which someone had once tried to grow vegetables but which was now covered in a top dressing of waste paper and rubbish of the kind which filled the ditch outside. As he was ushered across this patch, the first rays of the rising sun caught the topmost edges of the fortress walls, rimming them in gold against the paling stars. Wayne was led over to the main building, beneath a series of arches, up a narrow stone staircase and into a first-floor room. It had a single barred window facing inwards on to the courtyard while the other three walls were windowless. The room was bare except for a large iron bedstead with a thin mattress, much stained.

"There you are," said Tewfiq. "Luxury. Your own room and with a bed, too."

"My own condemned cell, you mean," retorted Wayne

bitterly. Tewfiq grinned and went out, shutting the door. A key rasped in the lock, footsteps receded. Wayne went and lay down on the bed, his ears still full of the roar of the diesel engine, his clothes exhaling the smell of stale cheese, and his body still heaving and swaying like that of a sailor newly ashore. As the sun came up, sparrows began twittering from their holes in the stonework around his window, and he fell into a deep sleep.

Chapter 9

THE ARRIVAL OF the cassette at the U.S. embassy had produced exactly the effect Tewfiq had hoped for. Mrs. Bulkeley listened white-faced and then burst into tears when she heard her son sign off "love Wayne." She was escorted gently from the Ambassador's office and put to bed under heavy sedation. Mr. Bulkeley, on the other hand, was for the first time aroused to immense anger.

"What the hell do you imagine was going on when that recording was made?" he asked Vance Deedle. Wayne's gasps and weeping had echoed eerily in the high white room.

"Perhaps it was an act which they staged somehow to add realism and make their point more forcefully," suggested the Ambassador hopefully. He himself had been much shaken.

"Oh, come on, Deedle; I know my boy. That was real enough, for Heaven's sake. Do you imagine they . . . they were . . . ?"

The Ambassador nodded. "More than likely I'm afraid, sir," he said. "They're beasts, you know; complete pigs."

"Bastards." Then, after a pause: "That does it. I don't care if the U.S. declares war on Zibala. You've got to do something. If this is allowed to go on a moment longer, I shall hold you personally responsible, Deedle. We're through with pussyfooting now. I think my wife and I have been extremely patient, considering that is our only child being tortured." He pointed at the tape recorder on the Ambassador's desk. "As a U.S. citizen I am now demanding that you do something to save my son and that you do it *right now!*" Wayne Bulkeley Sr. was on his feet, slamming his fist down on the desk top. "I simply cannot and will not believe that the world's Number One power can't bring some cheapskate little republic of stone-age tentmakers to heel. You'll do something now, Ambassador, before you have your damned lunch."

"I was going to, Mr. Bulkeley," said Ambassador Deedle. "I agree entirely with everything you say. The U.S. has a lot of muscle to flex, and frankly I don't think it should be slow to flex it at moments like this. As a matter of fact I was in touch with Washington last night, and first thing this morning I received authorization to take 'all necessary steps' to secure your boy's release. That permits me to go as far as I need, short of calling in a preemptive nuclear strike." The Ambassador smiled grimly. "What I *do* have in my arsenal is a collection of economic weapons, thumbscrews, strangleholds, armlocks and general nasties which President Barzuq is not about to ignore."

Ten minutes later, the black Lincoln, its pennant flying proudly, leaped away from the Embassy with a double spurt of gravel. His last act before leaving had been to convince Mr. Bulkeley that it was vital to get a copy of the tape into the hands of the international press as quickly as possible. He pointed out that the sooner such emotive and persuasive material was used to mobilize world opinion, the sooner President Barzuq would be forced to back down. Wayne's father had at first been hesitant about having his son's tearful pleas transmitted across whole continents to the ears of millions of indifferent but sensation-seeking listeners; but he had finally given in.

When it was worth their while, international communications functioned very swiftly indeed, even if one end of the line was in al-Mazar. Late that Thursday afternoon

Bernard himself heard Wayne's recorded voice coming over the radio. The BBC, normally rather reserved about transmitting sensational material, broadcast the entire tape. It had been prevailed upon to do so by discreet pressures; Wayne was, after all, partly a British subject. In any case, most of the main news agencies had their own copy of the tape and foreign broadcasting companies without as many scruples would be sure to milk it for what it was worth. In any event Wayne's pleas were given world coverage. Even in countries where a translation was needed, the cries of pain and the tearful begging spoke an international language. They caused a sensation.

At first Bernard was relieved to hear his friend's voice, strange and tinny though it sounded. Later, he walked from the room and was profoundly sick in the wash basin upstairs in his bedroom. Then he opened his wardrobe and selected a charcoal-grey suit he had been bought when the family went to Rome for his father's audience with the Pope. Next he stripped to the skin and, catching sight of himself in the full-length mirror inside the wardrobe door, examined his body without a trace of expression on his face. Then he dressed carefully in clean underwear, a crisp white shirt and a subdued tie. Finally he looked at himself once more in the mirror, examining the effect of the dark suit with his fair hair, still expressionless. Then he selected a clean handkerchief, closed the wardrobe door and ran downstairs. His mother, crossing the hall, caught sight of him.

"*Mon Dieu, chéri*, where are you going?" she cried.

"Out," said Bernard briefly.

"But, darling," began his mother and stopped herself. "Darling," she said, "I do truly believe he'll be all right."

"Oh you do, do you?" said Bernard. "That's nice. And what makes you think that?"

Slightly withered by her son's brutal tone, Renée Levesque offered: "Your father . . ."

"*Mon père . . . Mon père*," said Bernard, struggling to

say something. He changed his mind abruptly. "I'm taking Hassan. I shan't be long."

"But Bernard . . ."

Bernard went out through the front door calling for Hassan. Hassan was currently on loan from the Quebec Embassy as Mme. Levesque's driver, since the Ambassador had insisted that she should not drive herself while the kidnapping scare was on. Hassan came to life behind the wheel of her dove-grey Lancia, pulling on his cap and tucking his folded-up newspaper behind the sun visor. "Monsieur Bernard," he greeted the boy.

Bernard got into the back of the car, gave an order and drove away through the Residence gates. He was vaguely aware of, but indifferent to, the Zibalan police motorcyclist who swerved away from the curb and followed the Lancia watchfully from a distance of about forty meters. The car wound its way through the late rush-hour traffic towards the center of al-Mazar.

"Gentlemen," President Ismail Barzuq was saying to his Prime Minister and Cabinet at almost the same moment, "I'm afraid I have bad news for you. It is also bad news for Zibala. Early this afternoon I was given clear notice by the American Ambassador that the United States is firmly on the side of thugs, murderers, Communists and men of violence. He demanded that we give in to Seventh January."

The Prime Minister nodded. "I imagine we had all expected that," he said. "I presume it was a demand and not a request?"

"It was a demand."

"And what threats was he proposing?"

"The lot," said the President briefly. "You name it and he threatened it. Everything from mobilizing world opinion against Zibala and the Arab cause and guaranteeing vetoes in the Security Council to economic and military sanctions. No International Monetary Fund loans, all aid immediately cut off—bang goes your new summer residence on the coast, Wajih—" he said in an aside to the Minister of Public Works. "Zibalan exports blocked, no spare parts for any of our aircraft or tanks or weapons. I think that leaves us with sixty Russian crop-spraying planes and about five hundred buses in the event of a lengthy war, Mr. Minister?" The Minister of War nodded glumly.

"So you see, gentlemen," went on Barzuq, "we are not left with much option."

"Not a lot," agreed the Prime Minister. "Interfering imperialist dogs. I wish we'd gone nuclear."

"A great help that would have been," said Barzuq drily. "We could have turned the whole Jebel el Ahmar escarpment into a huge lump of fused glass."

"Well, that at least would have done away with Bir Huzun and those bastards hiding out in the hills," said the army officer who had interviewed Bernard after the kidnapping. "That's where they were, just as I said."

"You said they were in the south," objected the Minister of Security. "I distinctly remember."

"Pardon me but I said nothing of the kind. I never had the least doubt about where they were. But you know the situation in those areas as well as I do, Shukry; our hands are tied. They were there until last night, I'm certain of that. Who knows where they will have holed up by now. Why is this country so damned big?" he demanded petulantly.

"Gentlemen." The President held up a hand. "This is not getting us anywhere. The point at issue is, What do we do in the face of these American threats?"

"Give in," said the Prime Minister promptly.

"I agree," said the Minister of Public Works.

President Barzuq regarded his colleagues sourly. "What we will do is buy a little more time," he said. "Tomorrow morning I shall announce that the executions have been temporarily postponed. I shall wait until then because I don't want it to look to the U.S. as if we have given in with unseemly haste; there's a question of national dignity here. With, say, two or three extra days do you think you and the entire Zibalan army might find the boy and these terrorists?" he asked with a trace of sarcasm.

"No," said the army officer promptly. "Or if we did, we would still have our hands tied as before. It would be Bir Huzun all over again."

"Not this time," said Barzuq emphatically. "I'd rather take on a few thousand Bedou and the odd *rayyis qabila* than the United States. Besides, it will give the army some practice. Much-needed practice," he added.

"That's true," said the officer, suddenly enthusiastic. "Yes, sir, I do believe we can get these sons of dogs after all. You had better have the five prisoners appear in public some time, though, just to show Seventh January that their precious friends are still alive. After that . . ." he looked around gleefully.

"Exactly, gentlemen," said President Barzuq. "Then that's agreed. There remains one problem, however. There are only four of them left."

"I think we'd better get to the guerrillas before they discover that," said the officer. "Then if I have my way there'll be none of 'em left."

The Lancia dropped Bernard at the Roman Catholic Cathedral, a great gaunt building designed by the French in the last century. Once up the flight of stone steps and in through the felt-edged revolving door, Bernard found himself in sudden gloom and quietness, the late dazzle of sun and ceaseless hubbub of al-Mazar's traffic blotted out. He saw with relief that the place was empty. New office blocks had been built on either side of the Cathedral to within a few meters of its walls, dimming forever its rather gaudy stained-glass windows. But high above the nave a row of small clear windows let in a wash of sunlight, very remote among the neo-Gothic arches, in which motes of dust drifted in and out of visibility.

He walked slowly up the aisle, sniffing the agreeable faint odor of stale incense, his footsteps echoing hollowly in the emptiness. The closer he came to it, the blanker the High Altar seemed. From a side chapel a tiny flame glowing in a hanging red-glass lamp caught his eye, and he walked over. Nearby he found a basin of holy water and crossed himself as he had been taught; then he twitched up his trouser legs and knelt before the little altar presided over from a niche by a gilt Madonna.

Just inside the main entrance and watching Bernard through a glass panel in the revolving door stood his Zibalan police escort. If he was puzzled by these goings-on, he did not show it. He watched impassively until the distant boy stood up again, and then he walked back into the sunlight to his Russian motorcycle. Soon he started it and followed the Lancia back to the Quebec Residence.

"All in a day's work," he thought as he parked by the curb and watched Hassan close the wrought-iron gates at the entrance to the driveway. Beyond them he could see Bernard hurrying up the steps and going in through the front door.

Chapter 10

EXHAUSTED AS HE was, Wayne had slept throughout the day and the following night. He had been allowed to sleep on, presumably because at some mysterious moment he had changed from being a trophy into an inconvenience. He was awoken by distant cheering. It was still light, he saw, mistaking Friday's dawn for Thursday's dusk. He got up and went to the window wondering whose the voices were. With the light outside strengthening by the minute he realized that he had slept around the clock. With sudden panic he wondered what had happened in the day he had lost: for all he knew his death warrant had been signed on Thursday and this very dawn might be the next to last he would ever see. He vainly tried the door, hardly expecting it to be unlocked. He began pounding on it and shouting, and somewhat to his surprise Tewfiq himself appeared after a few minutes carrying a mug of tea.

"Awake, are you?" he said. "We've just heard some good news. Radio Zibala says that the executions have been postponed."

Wayne backed to the bed and sat down. "You mean your friends won't be shot tomorrow and so I won't be either?" His knees felt weak with relief.

"Apparently not. Mind you, we still haven't won; it's not over yet."

"Oh," said Wayne in disappointment.

"They said only that the executions had been 'postponed for technical reasons.' That's a face-saver if ever I heard one. 'Technical reasons,' my foot. I suppose they've run out of ammunition." He laughed sarcastically. "But it is the beginning of the end. It means Barzuq's under terrific pressure and he's beginning to break. I knew he would; I'm not surprised. You ought to have been awake yesterday: you wouldn't believe the uproar that recording of yours has created."

"It worked, then?"

"I'll say it worked. The foreign news services have been playing it for all they're worth: BBC World Service on the hour every hour, Voice of America, the Dutch, the French, the Germans, the Italians"—Tewfiq was counting off on his fingers—"the Swiss, the Scandinavians . . . You've no idea what an outcry you've caused."

"It wasn't me who caused it," said Wayne. "This is all your doing."

"Okay, us then. Together we've forced that donkey-President to back down. Not bad, eh?"

"I suppose," said Wayne. "So what now? Where are we, anyway?" he asked, glancing towards the window.

"It can't hurt to know," said Tewfiq reflectively. "We're near a village called Ghanem, on the coast about thirty miles west of Marietta."

"Oh." Wayne recalled having glimpsed the sea when they had arrived. "How long are we here for?"

"Just as long as it takes to negotiate a plane to fly our comrades and ourselves out of the country. Perhaps a day or two. Perhaps even this afternoon."

At his request to go to the bathroom, Tewfiq escorted Wayne downstairs and across a tiled patio to a tiny windowless cubicle containing, to the boy's surprise, a Western-style toilet. There was a dusty pile of the Zibalan semiofficial daily newspaper by the seatless bowl, and on the floor the glossy shards of a great many dead black beetles. Tewfiq waited outside the door and then took him back upstairs.

"Why do I have to stay in here?" asked Wayne peevishly as he was ushered into the bedroom again. "I won't run away."

"You certainly won't if you're in here," agreed Tewfiq, stepping outside and locking him in.

"How about something to eat?" yelled Wayne after him, beating on the wooden panels with his fists. He heard only a chuckle and then the sound of feet going down the stairs.

He spent much of the morning sitting on the windowsill, looking through the iron bars. He was not high enough up to see over the walls, so he had no idea how close the village of Ghanem was, nor how far away the sea lay. As far as he was concerned, his immediate world was that encompassed by the four tall walls of the fort. Now and again, one or other of the group would cross the sandy patch of ground below on some errand, and once Ibrahim squatted outside cleaning an old and blackened Primus stove. He got it going eventually, leaving a patch of sand which had been soaked with paraffin and then set alight. A thin column of dark smoke drifted upwards, and after a minute or two Tewfiq appeared and put the fire out with handfuls of dust.

He went back inside and reemerged with a live chicken. He was carrying on an incomprehensible conversation over his shoulder with someone inside—presumably Ibrahim. Tewfiq held the bird's head with one hand, and before Wayne had worked out what he was doing, produced a knife and sliced a deep gash in the chicken's neck just beneath its beak. Then, deftly transferring the flapping bird to his knife hand, he held it upside down by its feet and let the life drain out of it into the sand, still chatting to his unseen companion. Soon the weak spurts from the fowl's head became a thin trickle and its wings slowly stopped flapping as if it were being anesthetised. Presently it hung limp from Tewfiq's hand. He gave it a shake, like someone dislodging earth from the roots of a freshly pulled lettuce, and squatted down to pluck it.

As he watched, Wayne suddenly saw Tewfiq not as a guerrilla leader but as a peasant. Tewfiq might have travelled, might have studied abroad and learned fluent English; but as he hunkered in the dust with his knife thrust into the ground beside him, expertly pulling the feathers off the chicken he had just killed, he looked like any other Zibalan peasant Wayne had ever seen. He plucked and cleaned the bird in a couple of minutes and went back indoors, whistling.

Wayne judged that it was after midday when the man came upstairs and unlocked the door.

"There's food downstairs," he said. "You'd better come and have some."

Wayne followed Tewfiq eagerly, and there in a room with intricate wooden *mushrabbiyya* screens over the windows was a table on which were a large aluminum bowl of stew and a heap of rice in a pot. The other members of the group were already sitting on the ground outside, eating with spoons from tin dishes. There was a plate of green chillies on the ground between them. The stew smelled so good Wayne thought he might easily faint.

"Hungry?" Tewfiq asked him.

"I could eat a horse."

"It's chicken. I cooked it myself so I know. *Alhamdulillah.*"

"I saw you kill it," Wayne told him. "You've done that before."

"Many times," said Tewfiq, ladling stew into a bowl. "I was brought up on a farm, like just about everybody in this country."

"Where?" asked Wayne.

"You wouldn't know it. Down south, on the banks of our one and only river. Our house was made of mud bricks, like everyone else's in the village. *You* wouldn't have called it a house at all." He handed Wayne the bowl of rice and stew. "No glass in the windows, one split door and earth floors throughout. No electricity, water from the river in tins so that everyone had bilharzia and no drains other than the river from which we drank. Go ahead, *itfuddal*," he said to Wayne, who was standing with his spoon poised.

"You've come a long way from there," said the boy between mouthfuls.

"Not really." Tewfiq helped himself without hurry. "It makes a story. Maybe I will tell it to you one day. If we both live. *Insha allah*."

"Do you ever go home?"

"I go back to my village, of course. But the house I grew up in has long since gone. The river flooded one year, and all the huts melted. They have been rebuilt, of course, in much the same places. But my father wanted to put the new one a bit higher up the riverbank. Mind you, it looks the same: same size, same shape, same mud. We've been making them that way since they built the Tombs of the Hundred Kings at Ramla. Tombs!" said Tewfiq bitterly. "I sometimes think that's all Zibala has to show for the last five thousand years. This country is nothing but a gigantic burial ground. Millions of peasants just like my father, just like me . . . How's your stew?"

"Fantastic," said Wayne truthfully.

"*Alhamdulillah*. Have some more?"

Wayne shook his head. "I don't think I could," he said in some surprise.

"That's because your stomach has shrunk," Tewfiq told him. "You can make do with less now and you could go on making do with less, too, only I expect when this is all over you'll go back to stuffing yourself with those hamburgers and French fries and pints of ice cream. And now I want to hear the radio and know what President Barzuq is up to."

The news from Radio Zibala came at one o'clock. The announcer confirmed that the execution of the five imprisoned Seventh January guerrillas, due at dawn the following day, had been postponed for technical reasons. He went on to say that this decision had been reached as a result of legal and judicial difficulties and had nothing whatever to do with the attempts by certain foreign countries to meddle with Zibala's internal affairs by whipping up a storm of sensationalism over the Bulkeley kidnapping.

"Not much it hasn't," said Tewfiq sarcastically. "I really think we've done it," he added, switching off. Wayne thought the other men looked pleased although still tense. Clearly, the most difficult part was yet to come: negotiating their escape. Tewfiq explained that Daoud Hafez was back in communication and had himself been contacted by a member of the Zibalan Government.

"They're trying to get our plane organized for Sunday," he said. "Barzuq has agreed to get our comrades to Marietta Airport so that we can all meet there. It's a face-saver for him: Marietta's a very small airport and it is only used for internal domestic flights. There will be fewer unwelcome spectators for what will be a very humiliating eposide for Barzuq."

"I see," said Wayne. "How is it arranged, then? How do you know your friends really will be there? What's to prevent this from being a trick to lure us out of our hiding place?"

"There'll be sympathizers at the airport," said Tewfiq. "The police and the army won't know who they are, and they can't possibly hope to screen them out by then: they might be baggage handlers, tea boys, off-duty stewardesses, flight controllers, even the Airport Manager himself for all they know. The agents will contact us by radio when they have confirmed that our comrades are there. Then we make ourselves known to the authorities, and they'll send out a single helicopter with only one pilot on board to ferry us to the airport. When we get there we will land near the aircraft at a deserted part of the airfield. Our comrades will already be there, alone, or our helicopter won't land. After that we all climb aboard and take off. You will be coming with us because that is the only way we can be sure Barzuq won't try to double-cross us by hiding police on board or putting a bomb in the plane. It won't be a long flight, and when we get out the other end, I expect you will be flown straight back to al-Mazar."

Wayne nodded, licking his spoon clean of the last smears of gravy. "It's turning out quite well for you, isn't it?"

"It might be turning out a lot worse for you, believe me," Tewfiq told him drily.

"No, I meant Daoud Hafez getting back in touch like that."

Tewfiq did not reply for a moment, helping himself to a green chilli which he scrunched appreciatively.

"Maybe it was a bit of luck and maybe it wasn't," he said at last, but would not explain further.

The afternoon wore on. The men sat on the vegetable patch outside, playing with a pack of cards they had found and periodically listening to the radio. Wayne was given the run of the yard but had to remain in sight at all times. He wandered around, kicking at the sand and idly turning over the litter with his foot. There seemed to be endless corned-beef tins stamped with the U.S. Aid handshake, condensed-milk tins with the slogan "A gift from the European Economic Community: not for resale" and a good many sun-bleached Ramla cigarette packets. He felt most strange. He could hardly believe that the whole affair was coming to an end; but he could scarcely believe it had ever happened, either. He put his hand up and gingerly felt the healing lumps and cuts, the dulling tenderness of the weals on his throat. They were not imaginary, anyhow, and neither was the increasing looseness of his trousers.

"I'm bored," he told Tewfiq at last. "Have you got any paper here?"

"What for?" asked Tewfiq. "Paper darts with 'I am a

prisoner. Help' written on them? A letter to the newspapers? Your will?"

"I just want to draw," said Wayne. To his surprise Tewfiq produced a chewed pencil and a Zibalan school exercise book of thin, brownish and slightly glossy paper. Wayne sat down in a corner of the yard and became engrossed. It seemed that everyone had forgotten his existence because only when he stood up to stretch after an hour or so did Tewfiq come over.

"What did you draw?" he asked, looking down at the exercise book. He snatched it up and began leafing through it, laughing delightedly. "I must show them," he said, taking it over to where the rest of the group was still playing cards. "Look at these," he handed the book to Ibrahim.

Wayne had drawn caricatures of the Seventh January band, Tewfiq included. Some of them showed the men individually, others showed them together in group activities. There was one of Farid and Adil disgustedly making tea in the cave; a second showed them all huddled around the radio; a third depicted Tewfiq dressed as a Zibalan peasant dispatching a blindfolded chicken with a machine pistol at twenty paces. The men were delighted. They flicked over the pages, jabbing thick brown fingers at the pictures, howling with merriment. They were particularly pleased to recognize themselves, and even Farid produced a lugubrious scowl on catching sight of himself wearing desert boots and with a knife the size of a cutlass between his teeth.

"Where did you learn to draw like that?" asked Tewfiq with admiration.

"In school, it must have been," said Sami.

"No," said Wayne. "I didn't really learn anywhere. I suppose I taught myself. It's something to do."

"I reckon you deserve a cup of tea for that," said Tewfiq decisively. "And just to show you that we're democratic terrorists, I will make it myself."

Wayne was surprised by the effect he had made with an hour's casual sketching. The men's attitude towards him had changed noticeably. Tewfiq even found a packet of weird biscuits with caraway seeds embedded in them which he distributed with the tea.

"Where did you suddenly get all this food?" asked Wayne.

"Come to that, whose house is this?"

"It belongs to the Zibalan Government now. It used to belong to an Englishman who was a judge in the Marietta courts in the days when Zibala was occupied by the British," Tewfiq told him. "Judge Wilkins, his name was, I think. He came to Ghanem one day and decided to build a house here to spend his holidays in."

"Oh," said Wayne, surprised. "I thought it was hundreds of years old."

"No, less than fifty. Perhaps it looks older because the stone here is so soft; look, it's like cheese—even sparrows can burrow into it. Old Judge Wilkins must have been a strange man, although a lot of imperialists who came to Zibala were like him. He thought he could reform the natives by giving them a fresh start and plenty of encouragement, so he planted an enormous grove of olive trees and another of oranges."

"I think I saw them the night we arrived," said Wayne.

"You probably did. They stretch from up here on the hill almost as far as the sea. The Judge believed that when the trees were big they could make the inhabitants of Ghanem rich. So at weekends and in the holidays he was out here helping the peasants of Zibala make their fortune while during the week itself he was in Marietta clapping them in jail."

"Did the villagers here make the most of the opportunity he gave them?" Wayne asked. "Are they any better off now?"

Tewfiq shook his head sorrowfully. "That's how Judge Wilkins thought; you and he have the same kind of minds. You are forgetting that he still *owned* the orchards. The trees still belonged to him even if the villagers were getting a share of the profits."

"I see," said Wayne blankly. "Anyway, what happened to him?"

"He died. Then after the British left, the Government here took over all foreigners' property so they got this house as well. Mind you, it's of no use to the Zibalan Government, stuck out here on the edge of the desert, and the villagers wouldn't want to live in it: they've got their own little houses in Ghanem."

"So Seventh January use it now?"

"Now and then we have," admitted Tewfiq, "although for obvious reasons this will be the last time."

"They left you this food, then?"

"When we came, we found a few stores, some ammunition and that chicken locked in the kitchen."

"You're very well organized," said Wayne in some admiration. He wondered how their arrival had been known about in advance.

"We have a lot of friends. That's the only thing that gives me hope in this country: that despite persecution, beatings, torture, executions and the rest, there are still thousands of peasants who will give us active support and help."

"Are the people around here Bedou?" Wayne asked. "Is it like Bir Huzun?"

"Exactly. This area is just as much out of bounds to Government forces. If they want to come in here, they'll have to negotiate with the Ibn Khass family or risk trouble they haven't the stomach for. It is peasants and Bedou like them who will one day bring down the Government of apes and dogs which rules Zibala."

"I hope you achieve what you want to achieve," said Wayne seriously. Suddenly, despite everything that had happened to him, he found himself wanting things to go well for this strange, intense man. Tewfiq's evident passion contrasted oddly with a country whose other inhabitants seemed to Wayne sodden with apathy, cynicism or hashish. Perhaps that only applied to the city dwellers of al-Mazar, he wondered. Or perhaps as a Westerner he had simply been mistaken all along. Certainly it meant something that ordinary peasants were prepared to risk so much.

Evidently Tewfiq himself felt a difference in Wayne for he shortly gave him permission to go where he liked in the house itself. This clearly caused awkwardness with Farid and Adil, but presumably Tewfiq must have pointed out that there was no real security risk. As Wayne had noticed, the house itself was built into the surrounding wall, its outside face entirely blank and without windows. The only possible escape route would be over one of the other three walls which were lower and accessible only via the roofs of the stables and outhouses built against them. In order to reach them a person would have to leave the house and cross the yard: there was no other way.

Perhaps this thought might have mollified Adil and Farid; but as Wayne roamed the empty rooms of the house and glanced out of different windows, he would catch the same apprehensive and scowling gaze as they sat on the ground outside and watched their prisoner seemingly wander his prison at will instead of being kept in a cell. Gradually Wayne made his way up through a succession of bare rooms to the top of the house, but he was disappointed to find that the third flight of stairs ended merely in a top landing. He had been expecting and hoping to find a way up onto the roof which beckoned him magically. Searching in one of the two top bedrooms, however, he came upon a door set in one corner by a washbasin, at right angles to the wall and leading to what from the outside looked like a narrow cupboard, only a meter wide but stretching the entire width of the room. The door was locked.

Wayne's first instinct was to go and ask Tewfiq for the key; but on thinking about it he realized he would never be given it. Probably the group had even forgotten that the staircase existed—if indeed it was a staircase hidden behind the wall. Maybe they would not even have a key, Wayne reasoned. He bent and inspected the lock. It seemed ordinary enough, clearly unused and somewhat rusty, but surely possible to pick. It was only the falling light and the lack of anything at hand with which to pick it which made him shelve his plans until the next morning. It was, after all, less a bid to escape than something to keep himself occupied.

That night he lay on his board-like mattress and wondered what he could use to get the door open. Then he remembered the bed on which he lay. Rolling one corner of the mattress up, he inspected the springing beneath. It was as he had hoped: a simple mesh of stout wire attached to the bed frame with small springs along its four outside edges. In the gloom he managed to work an end of wire loose, and flexing it until his hands began blistering, he snapped a length off.

Satisfied, he slipped it back under the mattress and was just on the point of falling asleep when what sounded like an angry argument broke out somewhere below. Whichever room the men were in it was too far away for Wayne to be able to understand individual words. He lay fearfully in the dark and listened. For all he knew the argument had nothing to do with him; and yet how often had he lain awake as a child in his bedroom and heard with the same inexplicable dread his own mother and father shouting at each other downstairs. Sometimes he heard the words, and in fact most of their arguments had not seemed to be about him in any way. Nevertheless the mere sound of raised voices and the occasional thud of a chair being knocked over were enough to bring on a panicky sense of guilt, as if he were somehow to blame. What he used to dread most was the moment when a door would open downstairs and his father's voice would shout up: "Wayne! Come down here! I want a word with you!" It was useless to pretend he was asleep and had not heard the summons. He would go down, shaking, and

become hopelessly involved, standing awkwardly in the
sitting room or the kitchen or wherever his parents were,
shivering in his pajamas somewhere between sleep and
tears.

Now, with a burst of sheer childhood terror, Wayne heard
a door slam open and the sound of running feet on stone, a
shout, feet slipping, and the first echoing rush of steps up the
stairs towards him. He lay rigid.

"Let go, damn you!" He identified Farid's voice.

"No!" shouted Tewfiq. "There's no point now!"

"I'll kill the little bastard! Didn't we swear we would?
Didn't you swear to kill him? 'Wallahi'! you said. And he was
your friend. Well, if you won't cut his dog's throat I will."

"No, you won't," replied Tewfiq. "He's too useful to us."

"He's damned well useless. He has been nothing but a pain
in the neck ever since we got him. I knew all along we should
have ditched him: he's brought us nothing but bad luck."

"Maybe so, but he's still our passport out of this country
and for the others as well."

More voices joined in the general hubbub at the foot of the
stairs. Above them rose Farid's, querulous and determined.
Wayne had gotten up, from an instinctive fear of being
found lying helplessly in bed should the door burst open and
Farid come in with his knife. He stood barefoot and
trembling with his back to the wall. For a while it seemed as
if the scuffle on the stairs were coming closer, but then it
receded. The footsteps shuffled away; the voices quietened.
A door closed, and they died completely.

Wayne went on standing there against the wall for what
seemed to him like hours, but downstairs all was quiet again.
After a while he crept back to his blanketless bed and,
trembling with cold and reaction, lay awake in the dark with
his knees drawn up to his chin. He half expected Tewfiq to
come up and explain, his voice calm and rational; but
nobody came. He went on staring sleeplessly into the dark
but must have fallen asleep eventually because when he

awoke it was morning and Tewfiq was standing in the doorway. He wondered how long he had been there.

"I suppose you heard all that business last night?" he said, and for an instant Wayne had to struggle to remember. Then he nodded, sitting up and swinging his legs over the edge of the bed. The stone floor struck chill on his bare feet. "We had just received a message from Daoud Hafez. According to an agent in al-Mazar, one of our imprisoned comrades has been killed."

"What?" Wayne was now wide-awake. "But why? Is it true?"

"The source is completely reliable, I'm afraid," said Tewfiq tiredly. "It's true enough. As to why"—he made a gesture—"who knows? Perhaps it was Barzuq's way of showing he meant business and that the gains were not all going to be on our side. After all, it still leaves him with four lives to play with whereas we've only got one of you. I may say that certain people downstairs were all for doing away with you and taking their chances."

"I heard," said Wayne.

"So was I at first," Tewfiq told him.

"Oh," said Wayne. "Why didn't you?" he asked after a pause.

Tewfiq looked at him levelly. "Quite simple. You are still more useful to us alive than dead."

Wayne got up and walked to the window. Outside on the ground the others were grouped around the radio drinking glasses of tea. "Is that the only reason?" he asked.

"Of course."

"Have you ever done this before?" Wayne wanted to know. "Kidnapping, I mean."

"No," admitted Tewfiq. "Not kidnapping. Bank raids, yes; hijacking trucks, yes; sabotage and the occasional assassination, certainly. But never kidnapping until now. It has one danger which I had not thought would exist, and it increases every day that goes by."

"You mean the chances of being tricked?"

"No," said Tewfiq harshly. "I mean one begins to know the victim. That is fatal."

Chapter 11

IT WAS STILL early when there was a radio announcement that an aircraft would fly them all to Tripoli on Sunday morning together with the five prisoners.

"Damned stinking liars!" Farid sprang to his feet. "Five prisoners, by Allah. I don't see why we should believe a single word Barzuq says now." The others murmered agreement.

"No," said Tewfiq. "But we have to: we've got no option."

It was clear that last night's news had been a bitter blow to the group's morale. The atmosphere was so bad that although Tewfiq had left his door unlocked, Wayne preferred not to go downstairs. Instead he listened apprehensively at the window, invisible to the men immediately below him.

"Anyway, what took them so long to arrange the flight?" Ibrahim was demanding moodily.

"I should think Barzuq had problems negotiating with Libya," hazarded Tewfiq. "Anyway, it's done now."

"So he *says*. And if it's settled, why won't they fly us out today? I don't like it."

"I agree," said Adil. "I think it's very suspicious. Why the delay?"

"I don't know," said Tewfiq. He was clearly worried. "I don't like it either. But there's nothing we can do about it."

"Call Barzuq and tell him to rearrange it for today or else."

"Or else what?" asked Tewfiq. "At this short notice we haven't any bargaining power left. We've only got one hostage, and he can only be killed once. We're already stretching his life to make it buy us the lives of fi . . . four comrades, plus ourselves—that's nine—plus a free trip out of Zibala. It won't go any further."

"We could damn well start cutting toes off," said Farid.

"It wouldn't work," Tewfiq told him. "Time's too short. And I think Barzuq would almost be willing to take that gamble now. He knows we're not going to do any real damage to the boy."

"Who isn't?" demanded Farid.

"You're not. He's got to be alive and fit for tomorrow. We don't want to be hampered by a multiple amputee leaking blood everywhere. And in any case Barzuq could too easily retaliate by killing another of our comrades. Use your head."

"I still don't like it," protested Adil. "I think it's a trick."

"Okay, maybe it is. If they're going to use force anyway, they will simply wind up with our six dead bodies today instead of tomorrow. It's a gamble, right? We're betting that having got so far they'll let well enough alone and fly us out."

It was clear to Wayne that neither Adil nor Farid was at all convinced, and that everyone else was dubious. It was altogether an uneasy conversation, and he was glad not to be downstairs even though it had meant missing his morning ration of tea. He felt the men's aggression directed very much towards himself. He wished he could escape. Then for the first time that morning he remembered the piece of wire under the mattress. He retrieved it, looked at it for a moment as if deciding that he had nothing further to lose, and then crept quietly out and up the stairs to the top bedroom. Once there, he trapped one end of the wire in the door jamb and bent it into a short right-angled hook as his father had once shown him when they had lost the key to their garden shed in America. Much to his own surprise, after ten minutes' tinkering he managed to turn the lock. Something else Bernard could not have done without summoning the Marines, Wayne thought wryly as he pulled the door open. And there, just as he had hoped, was a flight of wooden steps leading upwards, the treads almost completely carpeted in dust.

He paused for a moment, listening apprehensively for sounds from below, but there were none. He went quickly up the stairs, the sound of his feet muffled. At the top was a plain wooden trapdoor. It had split in the sun, and through it Wayne could see a brilliant seam of blue sky. He tried to open it, but the hinges had rusted. Getting his shoulders under it he finally heaved it open and it fell back onto one of the many drifts of dust which, he now saw, lay about the unswept roof.

He climbed out. Beneath the sand underfoot, he could see that the area had been tiled. It was a simple large rectangle enclosed by a stone parapet the height of his chest. One or two thin pipes crossed it, supported on bricks, leading beneath a large wooden cover in one corner which was held down by chunks of stone: presumably a recessed water tank. The only other feature was a cairn of cemented stones near one corner of the roof, topped by a heavy metal peg. Wayne supposed that it might have been a mounting for a telescope through which Judge Wilkins perhaps surveyed his orchards stretching to the sea, or scanned the horizon for ships heading into Marietta, or maybe just star-gazed in the velvety Zibalan summer nights. He went to the outside wall and looked over the parapet.

It was a magnificent view. The gentle sandy hill sloped away, covered with more or less neat rows of trees, until it met a sea whose color he would have disbelieved in a painting. It was, he estimated, perhaps three-quarters of a mile away at most. Between it and the house there was a scattering of the familiar white flat-roofed houses among a group of eucalyptus trees—doubtless the village of Ghanem.

Inland, and on both sides, lay more of Zibala's seemingly unending supply of desert: scrub, rock, and sand alternating to the horizon. Only to the west was there any difference: a faint brown stain low down in the sky beneath which the town of Marietta presumably lay.

He crossed to the inward side of the house. As he cautiously approached the parapet, the tops of the other walls and then of the outhouses below came into view. Inch by inch he moved forward until his hands were resting on the stonework and with infinite slowness he peeped over the edge. He need not have worried. Sixty feet below him all five men were still sitting in the same place, the chrome antenna of the radio sticking up and glinting in the sunlight like a silver harpoon from their midst.

Wayne withdrew silently and crossed back to the other side. Resting his chin on his forearms, he gazed out over the landscape. He wished this were his own house. On such a secluded roof with no neighbors overlooking, he would acquire a suntan which would make Bernard himself look pasty and unwell, he decided. Like a parabolic mirror focusing the sun's strength onto a solar cell at its center, the roof would trap the rays and pour them into his body. There, alone on a towel in the middle, he would force his pallid skin to sweat and roast, sweat and roast, day after day until he was changed. He looked down at himself; he had definitely lost weight in the last week, perhaps as much as fifteen pounds. That was a real start. He vowed that whatever happened he would not allow the fat to creep back on again, would resist being stuffed like a Strasbourg goose. Full of good intentions, he drew himself up again and looked out towards the sea as if espying a new future.

At that moment the first notes of the *muezzin's* call to prayer floated up to him from the village of Ghanem half a mile away. *God is great. I witness that there is but one God. I witness that Mohammed is his prophet.* Wayne looked down towards the village, trying to discover which of the white walls partly visible among the trees belonged to the mosque. *Come to prayer. Come to success. God is great. There is no God but Him.* He leaned forward slightly in puzzlement. There were some curious outlines in the shadows cast by the distant eucalyptus trees: old lumps and humps which he almost thought he recognized. Suddenly he knew what he was looking at. Underneath the trees were parked several camouflaged trucks.

A movement in the orchard below attracted his attention. Although he was now half expecting something of the sort, it was still a shock to see individual men in desert-combat fatigues creeping from one tree to the next. Then he saw the whole hillside was alive with soldiers. They were wriggling uphill on knees and elbows, their automatic weapons held crosswise in their hands in front of them. The Zibalan Army had arrived.

Wayne's first instinct was to shrink back again out of sight, as in the cave when the helicopter had come over. But then he reminded himself that here, at last, was rescue and for the first time he could attract attention without immediately being shot. On the other hand, it somehow seemed a kind of betrayal not to warn Tewfiq and at least give him a fighting chance. As he stood in an agony of indecision he saw that he had already been spotted. One of the soldiers was waving urgently to him, making gestures which were perhaps inquiries about where his captors were. His mind made up, Wayne ducked back out of sight and ran across the parapet on the other side.

"Tewfiq!" he yelled. A ring of surprised faces turned suddenly up to look at him. "They're coming! The army's outside; they're crawling up the hill."

With a bellow of rage Farid leaped to his feet and ran to where his automatic weapon was propped against the wall nearby. "Bastard!" he shouted. "That son of a whore has betrayed us." He snatched up his gun. "Your precious passport to freedom has just sold us out!" he spat at Tewfiq as he sprinted past him into the house. From far below, the sound of his running footsteps came up to Wayne, the stairs taken two at a time, as Farid turned on the landings, coming closer and closer.

Fighting off that familiar paralysis of terror, Wayne crossed the roof, slammed the wooden hatch down and ran with lead-filled legs to fetch one of the heavy rocks holding down the cover of the water tank. But he was too late. He had just picked up the largest and was on his way back, holding it to his stomach and bent over its weight, when he heard Farid arrive at the top of the stairs. There was a thud and the hatch cover bulged, but evidently it had jammed again and it held fast.

Presumably Farid thought his intended victim was standing on it. Wayne heard a snarl of rage from beneath, and then an ear-shattering blaze of automatic fire ripped through it, blasting away the flimsy wood in a whirl of splinters. The bullets were followed by Farid himself who bounded up through the ragged hole, turned, and saw Wayne standing not three yards away still foolishly clutching the rock to his stomach.

"Now I'll have you, dog," said Farid with satisfaction. "Betrayed us, did you? By Allah I was right: I should have done this the first day." He raised the still-smoking barrel of the gun.

There was a long burst of fire. Numbly Wayne watched the muzzle of Farid's gun sag and sag until it dangled downwards from the fingers of one hand. Then the hand opened convulsively, once, twice, the second time staying open at maximum spread, fingers quivering with the strain. The gun could be heard bouncing down the stairs beneath him. Then slowly Farid made a slight turn, his hand relaxed, and he folded up with a little cry, plunging through the hatchway after his weapon with a series of heavy thuds.

In a few seconds Tewfiq emerged carrying his own gun and found Wayne still standing as if now paralyzed, his arms still gripping his rock. Suddenly Wayne let it drop with a crash.

"You . . . you shot him?" he managed to say. His teeth began chattering.

Tewfiq nodded brusquely. "We still need you, damn you." He moved swiftly to the parapet and looked cautiously over. Immediately there was a shout and a burst of firing from the ground, several bullets knocking chunks of sandstone into the air and ricochetting away overhead with shrill screams. Tewfiq quickly moved back.

"I didn't betray you," Wayne was saying. "Honestly I didn't, Tewfiq. They were there already. I . . ."

"Quickly!" Tewfiq grasped his arm and urged him towards the hatchway. "Get downstairs!"

"You must believe me," said Wayne. "I didn't betray . . ."

"Who cares if you did or you didn't?" broke in the man harshly. "What does it matter? They're here—that's all that counts. Come on, get down."

He pushed, and Wayne half fell down the stairs, unable to stop himself from treading heavily on Farid's body which was sprawled head downwards on the stairs. He managed to break his fall with the wash basin in the bedroom; then he felt Tewfiq grasp his shirt and propel him across the room. "Come on," he said, "we haven't any more time left. We'll be needing you as a shield."

They ran down the stairs. "Whatever happens," said Wayne as he crossed one of the landings, "you must believe that I didn't betray you."

"That's good," said Tewfiq, his voice indifferent and preoccupied.

"You don't believe me, do you?" cried Wayne.

"Oh shut up about it," ordered Tewfiq. "You're so damned sentimental. Just get a move on."

At the bottom of the stairs they found the courtyard empty. Then one of the men shouted, and looking in that direction, Wayne could see the stubby gun muzzles sticking out of various windows facing the high wooden doors of the main gateway. Tewfiq propelled him through the house towards them.

"This is it, then?" Adil asked, slapping the magazine of his weapon and moving its fire-select lever from Single to Burst.

"They shot at me on the roof," Tewfiq said. "They heard Farid fire at something up there so they probably think the boy's dead. Get Ibrahim to take his shirt off and wave it and tell them the kid's still alive. Say that if they rush the house Wayne will be the first victim and that's a promise." Adil nodded and ran through to Ibrahim. Tewfiq pulled Wayne back to the foot of the stairs and from beneath the stone archway they watched Ibrahim clamber across the roof of the stables, his shirt wadded into a ball in one hand. Then, crouching below the stone coping, Ibrahim waved the shirt above the edge for several seconds. When no shots came he rose slowly on his knees.

"The boy's still . . .!" he shouted, but they were the only three words he managed to get out. A single shot knocked him backwards onto the sloping stable roof. He slid down a little way, his muscular brown torso streaked with blood, his shirt still grasped in one outflung hand and blotched with red. He came to rest on the edge, his legs awkwardly doubled up beneath him.

"O Allah, the bastards," said Tewfiq softly. Two heads appeared above the edge of the wall, and immediately all three men fired long bursts which sent up clouds of dust and chips from the stonework. The noise was deafening, and Wayne stood by foolishly as a cascade of hot brass cartridge cases rattled around his feet from Tewfiq's gun, a cloud of cordite smoke drifting around him. The two heads disappeared abruptly, but whether from injury or prudence it was impossible to tell. Tewfiq unclipped his spent magazine and tossed it aside.

"Sami!" he shouted. "Go and fetch the spare ammo. We're all using too much. How much do you have left?" he asked as Sami passed them at a run.

"None," the man called back.

"Adil?" Tewfiq shouted. "How much have you got?"

"About half a magazine. And you?"

Tewfiq patted his pockets as if he expected to find one of the long curved magazines concealed in a pocket he had overlooked.

"Damn all," he called back. There came a sudden shout from Sami.

"We're finished," he said, running up to them, his hands full of ammunition boxes. "This is all nine millimeter. Every last box. Didn't you notice?"

Tewfiq ripped the lids off the boxes, greedily pulling out handfuls of rounds like a pirate with a chest of doubloons. Then, as if finding that the coins were all fake, he sat back on his heels, the bright brass and copper falling from his hands.

"I never checked," he said quietly. "I deserve to die for that. I knew all our guns were 7.62 mil. I—"

A sudden burst of firing came from the wall, answered almost immediately by Adil. A soldier collapsed on the coping, toppled, and fell heavily to the ground by the stables, his own rifle coming down beside him. A whoop of delight came from Adil. Wayne noticed that he alone was still on his feet. Sami lay behind a pillar to his left, apparently unhurt since he was getting up. Then there was a groan from behind them. Turning, Wayne found Tewfiq crumpled against the wall, one foot twisted and surrounded by a growing pool of blood. Sami was by him at once, ripping off his belt and making a tourniquet below his leader's knee.

A curious energy seized Wayne. At first the firing and bloodshed had seemed quite unreal: he had been a spectator watching a pageant or a film rather than a hostage whose life was being bargained with. The sight of Tewfiq lying helpless pricked him into having to act, into taking part. A noise overhead made him look up. A helicopter was edging over the house at a safe altitude. Panicked and without a thought, Wayne found himself running across the dusty yard, his bare feet oblivious to the open sardine tins and clumps of prickly pear. As he ran, he thought he heard Adil shout from his window and then a click which could have been that of a firing pin falling uselessly in an empty chamber. Then he had reached the wall on the far side, snatched up the self-loading rifle which lay by the body of the shot soldier, and ran in under the protective roof of the stable.

The helicopter was now directly over the house and practically motionless in the sky. Peeping out, Wayne could see an observer looking down through the open doorway with a pair of binoculars. Almost immediately the helicopter edged slightly away and there was a sudden electronic howl nearby. Wayne saw that the blank mouth of a loudspeaker had been propped on top of the wall facing the house. The howl rose to a scream which was cut off abruptly. A man's voice spoke boomingly above the noise of the helicopter's engine.

"Men of the Seventh January!" he said. "Hold your fire and listen. Your position is quite simple. You are surrounded by one hundred and fifty troops, and you have no hope of fighting your way out. We have seen the boy"—Wayne glanced instinctively upwards—"and we know he is still alive. Send him out, and we solemnly promise you all a fair trial." The voice stopped and was replaced by a loud hum from the speaker. Above it Wayne became aware that someone was calling him from the direction of the house. It was Tewfiq, who had dragged himself over to where Sami had been lying behind the sandstone pillar. Of Sami himself there was no sign.

"Wayne!" Tewfiq called again.

"Yes?"

"Throw me that rifle you've got."

Wayne stared foolishly at the weapon he held. He could not remember exactly why he had run across and retrieved it; he no longer knew whom to attack and whom to defend.

"Why do you want it?" he called suspiciously.

"Allah!" Tewfiq's voice rose despairingly as if he were in great pain. Then he said in more normal tones: "It's not to shoot you, I promise. *Wallahi*. I have sworn. It's all over now."

"You once swore the same oath that you would kill me."

"I know. I have failed. I was too soft and now it is too late; I could not possibly kill you. Now throw me the gun."

Wayne once again experienced the dilemma he had felt on the roof. Decisions of this sort were usually made easy by clear loyalties; but to whom did he feel loyal—the man who had kidnapped and beaten him or his unknown rescuers?

"Please!" urged Tewfiq again from his hiding place. "There is very little time left."

Suddenly, impulsively, Wayne hefted the gun and threw it as hard as he could in Tewfiq's direction before bolting to the back of the stable and standing behind one of the columns which supported the roof. Evidently the excitement of the moment had lent him strength: the rifle fell directly in front of the house, skidding half onto the tiled floor under the arch and coming to rest about ten feet from where Tewfiq lay. Wayne watched apprehensively as Tewfiq began dragging himself painfully towards the weapon. Then Sami emerged from the shadows, darted forward, snatched it up and thrust it into his commander's hands.

Then with horror Wayne saw Tewfiq struggling to point the muzzle of the weapon at his own body. The cocking handle had snagged on his jacket, and he could not quite get the weapon down far enough. Unthinkingly Wayne broke from his cover shouting to him to stop, but he was too late. Tewfiq had disentangled the weapon, calmly put the muzzle in his mouth and pulled the trigger. From the middle of the garden where he was, Wayne distinctly heard the click of the firing pin as it fell.

"Empty," said Tewfiq in a resigned voice. He laid the weapon down and pushed it slowly away with his fingertips.

He looked up to see Wayne standing barefoot among the rubbish. "Go on," he said, "get lost." But Wayne kept standing there. "Beat it!" Tewfiq shouted with his remaining strength. "Go! It's over. You're free. Finish." He closed his eyes tiredly and put his head down on his arms.

"I can't," said Wayne; and he was still standing there when the helicopter, which had never been far away, clattered overhead very low. Two Zibalan soldiers dropped over the wall, rifles at the ready, and backed to the main gates. While one threw the heavy bolts, the other covered the house, his rifle levelled and waiting. Then the gates opened and soldiers poured in. Three of them at once surrounded the motionless Wayne while the others quickly rushed the house and presently emerged with Sami and Adil. Not a shot had been fired. There was evidently no question of a stretcher for Tewfiq: the guerrilla leader was simply pulled and pushed along in the midst of a throng of soldiers, goaded on with rifle butts, his smashed foot dragging.

At this moment the helicopter pilot decided to land by coming in low over the garden, and everybody drew back and flung up protective arms as its downdraft whipped up a stinging storm of sand and refuse. Then it had vanished over the wall, and hands came down from faces. The dust cleared, and there stood Tewfiq, Sami, Adil and their captors in a diminishing snowstorm of feathers, and Wayne remembered the bird Tewfiq had killed for their stew. The caricature Wayne had drawn of him executing it was itself lodged face upwards on a nearby prickly pear.

"It wasn't me who betrayed you," Wayne said in a small voice as Tewfiq was led past him, but the leader's face was grey with pain and his eyes never looked up from the ground. The last Wayne saw of the group's remaining members was their being bundled into the helicopter which had landed about fifty meters away. Then he was surrounded by laughing, chattering Zibalan soldiers all trying to shake his hand at once.

Chapter 12

APART FROM HIS fantasy about the food he would eat when he
was released, Wayne had never thought very much about
what it would be like after he had been returned to his family
and friends. Had he given it some thought he would at least
have realized that he had become a famous figure: his voice
had been heard by millions and his case had been discussed
in cabinets and boardrooms throughout the world as other
governments and companies tried to work out what they
themselves would do if such a situation happened to them.
He had vaguely expected some newspaper reporters and
maybe a photographer or two, but nothing like the crowds
which began massing through the gates of the U.S. Embassy
in al-Mazar shortly after his arrival.

A second helicopter had whisked him back to the capital.
On the flight a Zibalan medical orderly had broken out the
first-aid kit and tried to clean up some of Wayne's more
obvious wounds. He was an enthusiastic young man, and
Wayne eventually stepped out of the chopper covered in
bandages from beneath which burst wads of cotton liberally
splashed with mercurochrome, the Zibalans' favorite antiseptic. The brilliant red stains and blotches added considerably to the general effect, and a gasp of horror went up from
his parents and the American Ambassador when they caught
sight of him. They had just driven across town at breakneck

speed as soon as they learned of his rescue and had expected
to find a tired and perhaps slightly grubby boy overjoyed to
be free. What they actually saw looked like the glum victim
of an appalling train disaster, barefoot and clearly bleeding
profusely.

"Medic!" Vance Deedle took charge, snapping his fingers
to summon the Embassy doctor whom he had thoughtfully
brought along. The doctor sprang forward while Ambassador Deedle pried the Bulkeleys away from their
offspring.

"It's okay, son," the doctor told Wayne, finding an
unbandaged arm and supporting him with such vigor that
Wayne lost his balance, which had anyway been temporarily
upset by the flight, and they both crashed to the floor. A cry
went up, people surged forward, cameras clicked.

"Oh no, he's dead!"—"No, he's only fainted."—"He's
terribly injured, poor lamb. I'd like to get my hands on the
bastards who did it. I'd give 'em Seventh January."

On the floor Wayne and the doctor disentangled
themselves, Wayne's face bright with embarrassment. "I'm
all right," he said angrily. "I'm not hurt; I can walk. Just leave
me alone."

"Now you lie there," the doctor persisted, "and we'll soon
get you out of this." But Wayne was already on his feet.

"I'm fine," he said firmly. His parents clinched with him
again. The cameras flashed and whirred.

"Let's go," said Ambassador Deedle. "Sure he's fit to
travel, Doc?"

The photographers followed them in a throng until they
were in the Ambassador's Lincoln. Then they milled around
the car like cattle inspecting something in the middle of a
field, faces and lenses pressed up against the smoked glass of
the windows. The Ambassador gave an order and they
moved off, gently nudging the human herd aside. Then the
questions started.

"Are you all right, son? He's so thin; look at the boy, he's skin and bone. Didn't they give you *any*thing to eat? Where did they take you? Did you ever hear a radio? Were they very violent? Were you actually beaten? *Where are your nice boots?*"

Wayne did his best, but something was wrong. He felt no sudden upsurge of relief to be back, of overjoyed affection on seeing his mother and father again. The fact was that none of it seemed at all real: no more and no less real than having been involved—a bare hour ago—in a violent gun battle. He experienced again the strange conviction that he was only ever a spectator. Nothing ever happened except on the far side of a sheet of plate glass.

He stared out at the familiar midmorning crowds of al-Mazar: at the country people in their robes, at the middle classes in their Western clothes, at the beggars, the match sellers, the boys driving donkeys or leading blind men, at the people simply sitting smoking hubble-bubbles or playing backgammon, at the people simply sitting, while around them and among them swirled the battered city traffic in an endless hooting stream. Still, he thought, there was the pain; that had been real enough. Unconsciously his fingers strayed to touch the bandage on his cheek.

"We'll have a look at that in just a couple of minutes," said the doctor, who was eyeing him from over the back of the seat in front, half turned with one shirtsleeved arm dangling down, the light catching the heavy gold signet ring as it swung with the car's motion. Indeed, no sooner had they arrived than Wayne was hurried off to the doctor's office.

"Okay now, let's give you a thorough going-over," said the doctor eagerly. "My, what an experience you've been through." It was clear that he, at least, was enjoying himself. Wayne stood or lay passively, breathing deeply and flexing various limbs as required. The doctor tut-tutted over his bandages as he removed them.

"Good grief," he remarked. "Terribly amateurish . . . And just look at all that mercurochrome. Where were they *trained*, these peasants, that's what I should like to know."

Wayne thought of the earnest young medic who had bandaged him, with his brown hands and his fumbling attempts to manage a large bottle of antiseptic in a helicopter bucking about in the thermals off the desert. He felt suddenly protective of the Zibalan. He, too, had probably come from a village like Tewfiq's.

The doctor was writing something on a pad. "Nasty graze on the head," he remarked. "How did you get that? And that cheek of yours is a bit of a mess, isn't it, son? H'm. The lip . . . open a bit wider if you can, I know it hurts. Good, good; excellent. Well done." He turned once more and made another note. Then he caught sight of Wayne's throat.

"What in hell did they do to you? I haven't seen a bruised throat like that since that attaché's wife . . . um, not for a good many years. That's terrible. A clear strangulation attempt, I should say, from the look of it. Tried to kill you, did they?"

"It was an accident," mumbled Wayne. The doctor raised an eyebrow.

"A likely story," he said. "Come on, son, you needn't be afraid anymore. They can't hurt you now; you're safe. One of them tried to kill you, didn't he?"

"It was an accident," repeated Wayne stubbornly.

"I see," said the doctor. He jotted something else.

"What are you writing?" Wayne asked him.

"Oh, this and that," said the doctor vaguely. "A sort of checklist of the damage. I expect they'll need it for the trial. Now let's have the remains of that shirt off."

It was a long, embarrassing session ending with Wayne lying nearly naked on the doctor's examination couch with a nurse washing and dressing his cut feet.

"A dreadful thing," she kept saying as she sponged the grains of sand out of the wounds. Wayne lay still and said nothing, staring up at the ceiling while the doctor sat at his desk writing busily. When the nurse finished, the doctor asked her to slip next door to the dispensary and handed her a list. When she had gone, he asked:

"Did you get any sleep?"

"Oh, yes," said Wayne. "Actually I slept quite a lot towards the end. It's very boring being a hostage, you see," he explained. "There's nothing to do but sit and wait."

"What did you do all the time?"

"We talked a bit. I drew some pictures. They amused Tewfiq and the others, at any rate."

"Tewfiq?" asked the doctor.

"He was the leader of the group," Wayne explained.

"Brutal, was he?"

"No, I wouldn't say so." Wayne considered for a moment. "No more than he needed to be. Tewfiq's all right," he added.

The doctor appeared dissatisfied with this answer, but at that moment the nurse came in bearing a tray on which was a collection of bottles.

"Ah," said the doctor. "Your medication. Soon have you on your feet again, young man."

"But I'm on them already," said Wayne, standing up gingerly and wincing. "There's nothing wrong with me except a few cuts and bruises."

"I think we'll let me be the best judge of that, don't you?" said the doctor firmly. "Now—" He selected a bottle off the tray. "These are antibiotics to stop your wounds infecting." He took another. "These are analgesics to take away the pain. These little ones"—he shook a brown phial—"are to help you to sleep. The fat ones are multivitamins—you're looking a bit peaky. What are these? Oh, yes, sedatives to help you calm down a bit after all the strain and excitement. Anyway, it's all written on the labels. I'll give them to your mother to take care of."

"Thanks," said Wayne blankly.

"It has been a terrible ordeal, I understand," the doctor assured him, clapping him on one shoulder. "As a matter of fact I think you stood up splendidly. I'm most impressed."

The word made Wayne wonder who had last used it and when. Then he remembered that Tewfiq had said the same after his abortive effort to escape to Bir Huzun. In Tewfiq's mouth the word had been praise indeed.

After the medical inspection Wayne was reunited with his parents. Ambassador Deedle was dispensing celebratory drinks to everyone who tried to cram into his office, but when Wayne appeared he shooed them all out with some difficulty.

"Well, young man," he said at last, "you sure caused us a headache. What can I offer you?" He glanced at Wayne's parents. "Beer? Something stronger?"

Wayne accepted mango juice and was subjected to questioning for the next half hour. Eventually the buzzer on the Ambassador's intercom sounded, and he took a telephone call.

"I'm afraid there are one or two more things we'll have to ask you to do," he told Wayne apologetically when he had hung up. "I know the doc's given you a clean bill of health, but you may not be up to it yet."

"I suppose that depends on what it is."

"There's some bigwig from the police who wants to have a word with you. Just a few questions about your kidnappers and where you were taken, I gather. You needn't if you're not feeling like it; I can simply tell them that the doctor won't allow it for a day or two. Naturally, your parents and I will be present: there's nothing to fear."

"Oh, all right," said Wayne. "I don't mind."

"Good lad."

Not long afterwards, a Colonel Darwish was announced. He was extremely fat and perspiring and mopped his face with a silk handkerchief as he came in. After introductions he impulsively leaned forward and shook Wayne's hand a second time.

"*Mabrouk*," he said. "Congratulations. Good luck. Very

good. Well done. You are back with us, *alhandulillah*. I offer
my deepest apologies that such a thing should happen to you
in Zibala." He shook his head and mopped his face
contritely. "My country is ashamed. That such men . . ."
Words failed him and he shook his head again. "But such
things are happening everywhere now, even in America," he
added, looking pointedly at Ambassador Deedle. The
Ambassador gave a small rueful nod but said nothing.

"Anyway," went on Colonel Darwish, "we wish to know
as much as possible about your experience so that we can
guard against such a thing happening again. For a start,
could you tell us the whole story?"

So once more Wayne recounted the week's events while
the others listened, his mother every now and then
punctuating his narrative with small gasps of horror and his
father with murmurs of "Doggone" and "I'll be a
sonofabitch."

At the end Colonel Darwish, who had been making notes
on a pad, asked for more details. What names had the group
used? Where was the Land Rover hidden? Exactly where
had he been taken? Had the group had any outside help? For
instance, had he seen the drivers of the two trucks which had
brought them to Ghanem?

Suddenly Wayne became reticent. The details were
nothing which could not have been verified easily by other
means, but as for the people who had been sympathetic to
the group . . . He thought of Ahmed and his dead father
and shook his head.

"Nobody helped Tewfiq and the others," he told the
Colonel. "It was all done by radio contact with this Daoud
Hafez person who is outside the country." The Zibalan
nodded, watching him closely. "There was nobody else."

"You never saw anybody bring the group supplies in the
cave?"

"Never."

"And what about those truck drivers?"

"I never saw them," said Wayne. "It was too dark."

"But it was dawn when you arrived at Ghanem, I thought you said." He peered closely at his notes.

"Not quite. It wasn't light enough, anyway."

"I see. And what about at the house in Ghanem? Did you see who brought the food?"

"No. It was there when we arrived."

"Oh. How do you know that?" asked Colonel Darwish.

Wayne shrugged. "That's what Tewfiq himself told me. I certainly never saw anyone."

"There, Colonel," broke in the Ambassador, who must have felt that Wayne was being harried. "I think the boy's had enough."

"Of course, of course." The Colonel shut his notebook with a show of accommodation, but he was plainly not quite satisfied.

"What will happen to Tewfiq?" Wayne asked him.

"They will all be tried, of course. They will get a fair trial as we promised."

"And then?"

"Oh," said the Colonel, "sentencing is right out of my line of business. That's a matter for the Judge. But you needn't worry, I can promise you. Zibalan law is quite clear about kidnapping used as a political weapon. Nobody need fear that they will get off lightly," he added grimly.

"I'll bet," murmured the Ambassador.

"They won't be shot, will they?" asked Wayne in alarm. "I don't want that. I mean, they didn't kill me, did they? They're not really criminals, either, especially Tewfiq. After all, they just want the best for the Zibalan peasants. I should have thought that was what the Government here wanted, too."

The Colonel looked around at the others. "You see how persuasive they are?" he said. "It's always the same with these Marxists: they concentrate on the ignorant and the children and brainwash them."

"I'm not a child and they didn't try to brainwash me," said Wayne firmly. "Nor are they Marxists. Tewfiq simply told me what Seventh January are trying to do about all the poverty and unfairness here. They kidnapped me to get their friends out of prison, not to get money for themselves like most kidnappers."

"Sure, son," said Wayne's father. "We understand. That's what they told *you*. As a matter of fact Daoud Hafez stood to gain one hundred and fifty thousand bucks."

"But he didn't order Tewfiq to kidnap Bernard just so that he could get money for himself," cried Wayne.

"Didn't he?" asked the Ambassador quietly. "How do you know?"

"Because," said Wayne in desperation, "Tewfiq and the others *wanted* to rescue their friends in prison. That's all they ever talked about."

"Perhaps," agreed the Colonel without conviction. "Although it may interest you to know that only one of them was known personally to any member of your group, and that was the man who unfortunately, er, died prematurely. He was the brother of this man you call Tewfiq."

"What?" cried Wayne.

"It's true. They were brothers. All the other four prisoners were common criminals, ignorant peasants who had been tricked by this Seventh January organization into committing murder and sabotage because they were told it would help Zibala's rural poor and hasten the revolution. They were nothing. They will pay the penalty. So will the rest. And now," said Colonel Darwish, hoisting his bulk to his feet and wiping his palms on his broad thighs, "I must go and report. Once more may I say how sorry we are that it happened at all, but how glad we are that you are safe and sound." He extended a fat hand to Wayne which the boy took unseeingly.

When the Colonel had gone, the Ambassador looked at his watch and said: "To hell with the press. They can wait until

tomorrow for their interviews. I don't think Wayne's up to it
now. We'll issue a statement instead. Now, what about a
decent shower and a large lunch somewhere?"

Wayne shook his head. "Just the shower, thanks," he said.
"I'm not really hungry at all. I think I want to go to bed."

"But darling," cried his mother. "You must have something
to eat. You've got a week's starvation to catch up on."

But Wayne remained firm. He was taken across to the
Residence and shown a bedroom.

"I'm sure you want a shower almost as much as you need
one," said the Ambassador's wife, covertly eyeing the week's
dirt on the back of his neck.

"I promise not to get into bed without having one first,
Mrs. Deedle," he said.

"Oh, I didn't mean that," she protested hastily. "What does
bed linen matter? It's only one set, after all. You do just
whatever you like. Good gracious, you're old enough now."

Left alone at last with a glass of water and five different
pills which the doctor had urged him to take, Wayne
showered luxuriously and stretched out on the bed, enjoying
the damp coldness of the sodden dressings which still
survived here and there. Everything seemed incredibly soft:
Mrs. Deedle's towels, her carpets, her bed. He lay back, his
pills untaken beside him. He could see no way of making
sense of any of it. Had Daoud Hafez just wanted money?
Had he counted on Tewfiq's risking everything to rescue his
brother? He did not know what to think. All he knew was
that he himself was safe and comfortable and that, however
many miles away, Tewfiq and Sami and Adil were
undergoing the sort of interrogation he refused to think any
more about. Wayne fell into an uneasy sleep. He awoke
hours later to see Bernard come into the room. He sat up
sleepily.

"*Mon Dieu!*" cried Bernard, "what did they do to you?"
He came over and sat on Wayne's bed. Not knowing quite

what to do, he stuck his hand out awkwardly in a French gesture, and Wayne shook it, feeling foolish. "Oh, Wayne, I'm so glad to see you," Bernard burst out suddenly. "I thought you were dead. I . . . they all prayed for you at school," he amended hastily. "The Chaplain stood up and asked us to radiate love."

Wayne laughed. "I bet he did," he said. "I can just hear him. 'Love,' " he mimicked the Chaplain's eager style, " 'is like nuking the Devil with atomic warheads. It's a punch he just can't roll with.' "

They both slapped the bedclothes in a kind of drunken release.

"I feel high," said Bernard. "You've no idea how good it is to have you back. You're a celebrity, did you know? I'm so envious . . . Golly, it has been really grim. Everyone hanging about the radio with faces as long as skis. We had a party the night after you were kidnapped. It was ghastly—a lot of complete jerks just talking about themselves and their careers, as usual. That's all they're ever interested in. But come on, tell me what happened to you."

"I want to know what happened to *you* after you went down the tower," said Wayne. "How ever did you manage to avoid being caught? I saw you from upstairs, you know." So they exchanged stories.

"What were they really like?" asked Bernard at the end. "Total beasts?"

"No. That's the trouble. Obviously, everyone wants me to say that they were, but they weren't. They were pretty tough and I was dead scared much of the time, but they were trying to do something which couldn't be done in any other way. Tewfiq was definitely not a beast. In fact, he saved my life several times when one or other of his men wanted to kill me. It was always Tewfiq who talked them out of it."

"He knew you were more use alive—that's why," said Bernard.

"Well, yes; that's what he said. Of course, it was true."

"Come on, it wasn't because he liked the color of your eyes."

"No, but there was something about him which I can't explain. At times he seemed almost sad; I know it sounds crazy, but I don't think he really liked being a guerrilla. It was more something he felt he had to do."

"Don't tell me," pleaded Bernard sarcastically, "he came from a broken home."

"I knew it would sound like that," said Wayne. "Really, all I mean is that he was angry about all the corruption and violence here. He didn't want to add to it."

"That's probably why he failed in the end—not ruthless enough. The guerrilla with the heart of gold. He certainly wasn't much of a soldier, was he? Think of having the wrong ammunition and sitting around all day without posting look outs. I'm damned glad he did fail because otherwise you wouldn't be here."

"True," admitted Wayne.

The next day, despite his disinclination, he agreed to be interviewed by selected members of the international press. Somehow, though, he was made to feel that he had all the star qualities of a first-rate news story but that he failed dismally to live up to expectation.

"It was awful," he said afterwards to Bernard. "It was as if they had already written their stories and were only waiting for me to fill in a few details. I couldn't agree with half the things they said. For instance, they told me that I had been beaten half to death and forced to attend Communist indoctrination sessions. So I told them it was simply untrue. I had been beaten a bit once or twice and I had asked what Seventh January were trying to achieve—that's all. But those idiotic newspapermen wouldn't listen. They had their theories, and they weren't interested in facts. They think I've been brainwashed, you know," he added seriously. "Everyone does. They kept smiling sympathetically and shaking their heads. And when I tried to tell them about the grievances the peasants have here, they just stopped writing and closed their notebooks. Would you believe, they weren't even interested that I had seen the army commit murder by throwing someone out of a helicopter? They said it was probably an accident in any case, but that nobody could ever prove it wasn't and the army will claim the man slipped. I can't make a real fuss about it because I don't want to identify the man's son. It's hopeless. The press are cowards and liars."

"Oh, come on," said Bernard. "What did you expect? It's a bit naive of you to come back and support the people who kidnapped you and expect newspapermen to listen: it's not what sells papers. They want juicy stories of humiliation and brutality so their readers can feel that warm glow of outrage. They don't want stuff about poverty and corruption in Zibala: they've any amount of poverty-and-corruption stories on file from all around the world. Nobody's interested. The odd peasant revolutionary who tries to take on a government and gets squashed is too boring. The reading public wants to know that you were raped at gunpoint for a week."

"But I wasn't," objected Wayne.

"You can still say you were," persisted Bernard. "After that recording of yours, everyone more than half believes you were. Why not? You'd make a fortune."

"I'll just have to stay poor and with my reputation intact, then. And anyway, there's masses of human interest in Zibala," and he recounted to Bernard some of the things he had learned from Tewfiq. But Bernard only shook his head.

"When the socialist movement—or whatever it is here— looks strong enough to be a real challenge to Barzuq or whoever's in power then, people abroad will start taking notice," he said. "Until then, peasant leaders like your Tewfiq are expendable. They're no threat. *Time* magazine might refer to them as 'hints of smoldering unrest' or some such cliché, but they merely turn into local martyrs and everyone else forgets them."

"I won't ever forget him," said Wayne.

"Of course not, after what you went through. But come on, *n'importe*," said Bernard gaily in an effort to cheer his friend. "Let's get out of this awful house and go and do something together."

"I suppose. What's today? Monday? Our day for riding at Ramla, I think."

Bernard laughed. "Now I know they haven't washed your brain," he said. "That's a real Wayne-type suggestion."

The idea proved less popular in other quarters. Ambassador Deedle groaned and put his head in his hands when he heard, but after much insisting Wayne got his way. The condition was that the two boys were shadowed by a couple of meaty Embassy men posing as uncles "in case," as the Ambassador put it, "lightning decides to strike the same place again just for laughs." Another person who initially went against the scheme was the *mudir* at the stables.

"Excellency," he cried, hurrying up to Wayne and seizing his hand. "You are safe again, you are back. *Alhamdulillah, alhamdulillah.*" He kissed the back of his own hand fervently and made a gesture towards the sky. He appeared scarcely to notice Bernard but plied Wayne with cold Zibacola and basked in the glory reflected by his briefly famous customer. Stable boys and one or two tourists gathered around as the *mudir* insisted on Wayne telling his story in full. Wayne made it as short as he could, noticing out of the corner of one eye an upstaged Bernard standing at the edge of the group scuffling his shoes absentmindedly in the sand. Eventually they extricated themselves and managed to induce the *mudir* to part with four horses. He put up a great show of reluctance.

"I have only one tiptop horse," he said regretfully. "Alas. Your horse—" he said to Bernard "—found its own way home that night. But yours—" he nodded at Wayne "—is still lame after your friend rode him back so fast. He nearly killed him," the *mudir* added.

"It was in a good cause," said Bernard coldly. "If I could have made it go any faster, I would."

"Do you think that trick the Arabs use in the Gulf works?" Wayne wondered later when, after considerable sums of money had changed hands, the boys set off towards Ramla followed at a discreet distance by their "uncles" mounted on two bony nags.

"What trick?" asked Bernard.

"When they want their camels to go flat out in races. They prick a green chilli with a needle and push it up the camel's ass. They're supposed to go like bullets."

"The things you know." Bernard shook with laughter. "Can it be true?" And he lapsed into a reflective silence until they reached Ramla.

Once there, it was immediately apparent that any attempt to recreate the previous Monday's atmosphere for the pleasure of a different outcome would be impossible. Whether by chance or because Ramla had acquired more notoriety, there were a good many Land Rovers drawn up by the Tombs and the postcard-and-Zibacola sellers were doing a brisk trade with parties of sweating tourists. It was most unusual.

"Let's go back," urged Wayne; but Bernard seemed reluctant to stop his horse from wandering closer. The thought crossed Wayne's mind that perhaps Bernard was hoping he would be recognized. Eventually Bernard went and bought four hot bottles of Zibacola for themselves and their "uncles" who were wilting visibly in their saddles and were, in fact, telling each other exactly how much agony this unaccustomed ride was going to cost them next day.

So they turned around and went home. Eventually Bernard said: "My father nearly got it wrong, you know."

"Got what wrong?"

"He said Barzuq would back down well before he actually did."

"Oh, well, he was right in the end," said Wayne.

"Um." Bernard seemed to be struggling. Then he said suddenly: "Promise you'll never tell anyone what I did?"

"Promise," agreed Wayne, full of curiosity.

"Would you believe it? I was in such a state I went and lit a candle for you in the Cathedral."

Wayne hardly knew what to say. He shot a quick glance at his friend, but Bernard was staring out over the desert away from him, shaking his head as if in self-mockery. His neck looked red. An image came into Wayne's mind of Bernard standing beside a statue of the Virgin with an attaché case in one hand and a confidential expression on his face. The caption underneath read: "Here, let me give you my card." Wayne smiled to himself.

"Thanks," he said, both embarrassed and touched that Bernard should at last have put himself at a disadvantage. "Perhaps it worked."

"Rubbish," said Bernard gruffly, thinking that the Chaplain had said something along the same lines. "Anyway," he said, changing his tone and the subject, "I'm afraid your bandit chief was a bit of a jerk; I've been thinking about it. What was that you told me he said? Something about Seventh January not being interested in economics. I mean, how naive can you get? What else does he think politics are about? In any case he was far too soft to be any good. He used personal emotion to make military decisions. If he had obeyed Hafez's order to release you, it would all have been different."

"Not very. His brother would still have been dead. But, yes, I think probably that most of his decisions were emotional ones. A bad guerrilla but a good man."

Wayne turned in the saddle and glanced back. Behind their plodding "uncles," the Tombs of Ramla were drawn up, shoulder to shoulder on the horizon. He thought of having watched them at sunset a week ago from somewhere out in the desert, little pegs as they had seemed then, symbolizing the home and safety he doubted he would see again. Now it was hard to think of these nearby towers as being the same ones.

"I don't understand any of it," he said half aloud.

But Bernard was not listening. "Do you know what that friend of mine Damian wanted?" he was saying. "He's got this hash . . ." He seemed to have recovered completely from his momentary discomfiture.

The following day Wayne asked if he might be allowed to visit Tewfiq in prison, but his request was turned down politely but firmly by Ambassador Deedle.

"Not a chance," he told Wayne. "Don't even think about it. The Zibalan authorities won't agree to that for one second."

"But you could try," pleaded Wayne.

"It wouldn't be worth even a try," the Ambassador said. "I know the people here. Some fellow like Colonel Whatsisname, Darwish, whom you saw on Saturday would get the request and reject it at once. This isn't the U.S.: They don't have prison visiting around these parts. Nobody would understand why on earth you'd want to see a guerrilla who had kidnapped you. And quite honestly, neither do I. I should have thought you wouldn't want to relive those experiences by setting eyes on any of that bunch of thugs ever again."

It was no use. Wayne even offered to give evidence at the trial. He was thanked courteously and told that luckily for him such an ordeal would not be necessary since the State Department had enough evidence to prepare its own case. Wayne explained that Tewfiq's lawyer might want to call him for the defense, but this was received with indulgent concern.

"A good long holiday and a quiet think is what you need,"

his father told him. "Get you away from this damned
country. MOPEC's posting us back to the States, didn't I tell
you? They're giving me a month to wind up things here.
Meanwhile, Mom has suggested that you and she fly to
England in a couple of days and spend some time with Aunt
Matty. Then you could join me in the States when I get home,
and we'd all be together again. How does that sound?"

There was nothing left for Wayne to say. Everything had
been organized and planned for him. Maybe Bernard would
keep his promise and invite him up to Quebec in the summer
where he was apparently joining some pop group on tour;
maybe he would not. Each day, as the expensive and
familiar machineries of travel, traveller's checks, farewell
parties, Embassy cars to the airport and first-class flights
closed in on Wayne, the almost reality of his brief encounter
with some desperate men who called themselves Seventh
January became almost a dream. Tewfiq's face haunted him.
It was never Farid with his knife and his bluster who
intruded on his sleep, but Tewfiq himself and particularly
the Tewfiq of the final day. He remembered the argument
which had broken out that last night at Ghanem when they
had had to restrain Farid yet again from running upstairs to
kill him. That had been when they heard that Tewfiq's
brother was dead. But had any of them known he was
Tewfiq's brother? Wayne wondered. What had Farid
shouted on the stairs? "He was *your* friend."

Three weeks later Wayne was waiting for a bus in Piccadilly
Circus. Compared with the Londoners who were passing, he
looked brown and fit. He was also very much thinner.
Suddenly his eye fell on the day's newspapers on a stand, and
he saw the word *Zibala* in the headlines. He went over to
look.

On the front pages of nearly all the papers was the same
photograph, but on that of an imported Arab newspaper of
the day before, it was very enlarged and detailed. It showed

a gallows in al-Mazar's Independence Square. Hanging from it were the bodies of seven men, all dressed alike in long white execution robes with their hands tied behind their backs. Their shadows in the bright Zibalan sunlight made dark puddles directly beneath them. Several of the bodies had turned away from the camera, perhaps in the wind or at the untwisting of a rope.

But the face staring sightlessly into the lens with its mouth slightly open was quite recognizable; and as if to ensure that there was at least one thing about which Wayne could be quite certain, one of the man's bare feet was bandaged.